Local Customs

Audrey Thomas

DUNDURN
TORONTO

Editor: Shannon Whibbs
Design: Laura Boyle
Printer: Webcom

Library and Archives Canada Cataloguing in Publication

Thomas, Audrey, 1935-, author
   Local customs / by Audrey Thomas.

Issued in print and electronic formats.
ISBN 978-1-4597-0798-6 (pbk.).-- ISBN 978-1-4597-0799-3 (pdf).--
ISBN 978-1-4597-0800-6 (epub)

1. L. E. L. (Letitia Elizabeth Landon), 1802-1838--Fiction. I. Title.

PS8539.H62L63 2014   C813'.54   C2013-902973-7
                                               C2013-902974-5

1   2   3   4   5   18   17   16   15   14

Conseil des Arts   Canada Council   ONTARIO ARTS COUNCIL
du Canada   for the Arts   CONSEIL DES ARTS DE L'ONTARIO

We acknowledge the support of the **Canada Council for the Arts** and the **Ontario Arts Council** for our publishing program. We also acknowledge the financial support of the **Government of Canada** through the **Canada Book Fund** and **Livres Canada Books**, and the **Government of Ontario** through the **Ontario Book Publishing Tax Credit** and the **Ontario Media Development Corporation**.

Care has been taken to trace the ownership of copyright material used in this book. The author and the publisher welcome any information enabling them to rectify any references or credits in subsequent editions.

J. Kirk Howard, President

Visit us at
Dundurn.com | @dundurnpress | Facebook.com/dundurnpress | Pinterest.com/dundurnpress

Dundurn	Gazelle Book Services Limited	Dundurn
3 Church Street, Suite 500	White Cross Mills	2250 Military Road
Toronto, Ontario, Canada	High Town, Lancaster, England	Tonawanda, NY
M5E 1M2	L41 4XS	U.S.A. 14150

To Sarah, Victoria, and Claire
And to the memory of Peggy Appiah
and Monty de Cartier

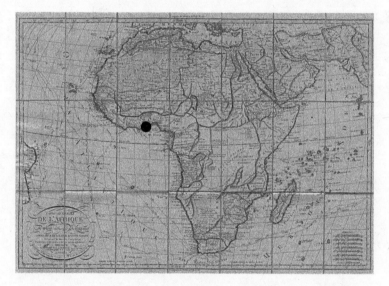

Carte Generale De L'Afrique by Eustache Herisson, 1829. Dot indicates location of Cape Coast.

Courtesy of the University of Texas Libraries, The University of Texas at Austin.

Duncan: "This castle hath a pleasant seat;
            the air nimbly and sweetly recommends itself
                    Unto our gentle senses."

                                        — *Macbeth* I, VI, I

            "Well," exclaimed Lord Harvey,
            who had appeared to be absorbed in
            watching his own shadow on the water,
            "I do not think it is such a dreadful
            thing to be married. It is a protection,
            at all events."
                                        — *Ethel Churchill*,
                                        by Letitia Landon

            "She no sick; she no complain, no nuttin'.
            And then she go die, one time."

                                        — *Isaac*,
                                        sense-boy at Cape
                                        Coast Castle

Letty: I can speak freely now that I am dead.

Prologue

MY NAME IS LETITIA ELIZABETH LANDON, nickname Letty, early professional name L., and later L.E.L. It was a shock to several of the young beaux at Oxford when it was revealed that L.E.L., who wrote such sweetly melancholic poetry was a young woman, not a young man. The initials had been my publisher's idea; they added to the mystery. I was also known, briefly, as Mrs. George Maclean, wife of the Governor of Cape Coast Castle, on the Guinea Coast. ("Mrs. Maclean as was," as Mrs. Bailey would say. You haven't met Mrs. Bailey yet, but you will.)

I say "My name is," not "was," because your name is your name and stays with you forever; it will still be my name a hundred years from now, two hundred, even if no one by then can remember why it was important. "L.E.L.? Wasn't there some mystery …"

I was born on 14 August 1802, the eldest of three children, a brother named Whittington and a sister who was an invalid and died young. Our father was a partner in the firm of Adair and Company, who supplied the army during the Napoleonic Wars. He prospered, but then lost most of his money on speculation and the romantic idea of a gentleman's hobby farm in the country. We became what I suppose one would call "shabby genteel," a family with a good name who had come down in the world. In spite of being the engine of our rapid descent into almost-poverty, I adored him. It was not his fault that he was impractical, a dreamer, and even less his fault that he died very suddenly of a heart attack. At a very early age I became the financial head of the family and it was lucky for us all that I was not only prolific, but popular.

They said I was a precocious child and knew my letters even before I could string them into words. Once I could actually read, nothing excited me so much as books. I was supposed to have been seen often rolling a hoop with one hand while holding up a book with the other, no doubt some romantic adventure. True or not, it paints a very pretty picture. I do know that I wasn't the least bit interested in most of the things a young lady *should* be interested in. I did no embroidery, did not sing or play the piano, never asked for a receipt or a pattern in my life; I was totally deficient in the science of the spoon and the scissors. What I excelled in was words, they flowed from my pen almost as though I had nothing to do with the actual composition; I simply had to be quiet and let them come in. Of course there were revisions — that's where the hard work comes in, that's the exhausting part.

I was considered a genius by some, a silly rhymester by others. I think I understood what people wanted, or some people, mostly, but not exclusively, women. I could definitely move about in Society and was welcome at the very best mansions. I was not a debutante, of course. I was never presented at Court in a white dress with the requisite three feathers in my hair, like some gigantic white cockatoo, but I was definitely part of the London literary scene without having to go through the rigors of The Season, or the "Meat Market," as some wag called it, where the real purpose of all those fifty balls and thirty luncheons and numerous dinners was to secure a suitable husband as soon as possible. If the Honourable Lady Annabelle Thing hadn't managed to be engaged by the end of her second season, she was considered a failure.

I was invited to select Wednesdays at men's clubs, where the men attempted to show us how well they could do without us, dining on greenish soup and overdone sole and some sort of pudding remembered from their nursery days; to the National Gallery; to walks in Hyde Park; to house parties in the country where one had to admire everything, from the park to the pigsty and where I never really had the right quantity of clothes for the many changes of wardrobe, but learned how to do wonders with a brilliant shawl and a smile.

I was good at being a guest. I liked talking; I looked charming when I talked. I liked strangers; every stranger presents a new idea. And I knew how to listen, how to make the person speaking to me feel as though he were the most important person in the room. That is a great talent and will take you a long way — even as far as the Gold Coast.

The following is the story of my meeting with George Maclean, our engagement and marriage, our life at Cape Coast Castle, my unexpected death. You will also meet Brodie Cruickshank, another Scot, like George, in charge of the fort at Anamaboe, who became my great friend, and Mr. Thomas Birch Freeman, a Wesleyan missionary, Mrs. Bailey and several other characters of interest.

The story takes place between 1836 and late 1838, in London and at Cape Coast, just before the rains end and the Dry Season is about to begin.

It is curious how much of its romantic character a country owes to strangers, perhaps because they know least about it. I will try, at least, to give some sense of what that world on the coast was like.

It is worthwhile having an adventure, if only for the sake of talking about it afterwards.

"AND WILL THERE BE LIONS AND TIGERS?" I asked.

"If you want those you must go elsewhere," he said, smiling at my ignorance. "But lovely birds, Letty, and palm trees, hibiscus flowers. The landscape is quite beautiful."

"I was rather hoping for lions and tigers," I said, but smiled up at him so that he would know I was only teasing, gave his arm a little squeeze.

I don't think I have ever walked so much as I did in the days of our courtship: Kensington Gardens, Hyde Park Gardens, Regents Park, Russell Square. In my plan of Paradise, I always said, people will ride very little but walk not at all. In revenge they shall have the most comfortable chairs from morning to night. But George was better outside; drawing rooms and gossip did not interest him. He would have fled London for the hills of Scotland long before, except for me.

He smiled at babies in perambulators, at little boys sailing their boats; I did not want him to look at babies or little boys; it was important that he keep his mind on me, on what he had been working up to say.

"I'm feeling a little fatigued," I said, spotting an empty bench. Just beyond, an old man was casting bread to the ducks.

We sat down. There was a not unpleasant silence between us.

"'Cast thy bread upon the waters,'" I said, "'for thou shall find it after many days.' I've never been quite sure what that means."

Still silence, but less comfortable. I wondered if I should suggest we continue our promenade. We made a pretty picture, Captain Maclean in his scarlet tunic and I in my new pelisse. I made a small movement, as if to rise, but he grabbed my hand.

"Letty," he said, "I have no flowery way to say this. Will you marry me? Will you come back with me to the Coast?"

Victory. (Bugles and pennants, but only in my head.)

"Of course I will, George." Then, "Shall we walk?"

Letty

I WAS THIRTY-FOUR when I first met George Maclean, and somewhat fearful and uncertain as to what my future was to be. Famous, yes, but solitary and I had recently noticed how some of my friends' children called me "Aunt." Soon those children would be having children and there would be another round of silver christening cups or porringers. Have you read Lamb's essay about Poor Relations? Would I end up like that, an embarrassment, an elderly lady living in a pokey room at my brother's house, his wife (I assumed he would marry now that his living was secure) treating me with condescension, his children (I assumed he would do the usual thing and have children) prompted to ask Auntie if she wanted the last tea cake or crumpet (Auntie declining even as her stomach rumbled). Or perhaps the Misses Lance would leave me their house when they slipped off their mortal coils, assuming old Mr. Lance, their brother, had already slipped his. I had a soft spot for old Mr. Lance. Whenever I was sent a gift of a brace of pheasants or a nice plump hare, he would remind us of what a crack shot he had been in his youth. The Lances did have nieces and nephews, so I probably could not really count on anything in that direction. If my brother didn't want me, perhaps I would live out my declining years in a pokey cottage, seeing no one, alone with my books, my canary, and a cat, until, if a traveller knocked, he would be greeted only by a whisper behind a door.

I had always declared I would never marry, but that is the sort of thing women say, isn't it, when they are no longer girls and still single. I didn't so much want a husband as want the security of a husband, the status that comes from being married. He would have to be a gentleman, of course (the Landons may have come down a bit in the world but we were of an old and respected Hertfordshire lineage). It would also be useful if he had a good income, but even an adequate income would suffice. I had my own money — from my books —

although I didn't see a great deal of it; as soon as it came, a goodly portion went out, to my brother, for his Oxford education, and to my widowed mother. There was a sister, sickly from birth, and she lived with my mother until the poor child died at age thirteen. You will be shocked, but at the moment I can't remember her name. An ordinary name, nothing like Letitia or Whittington, my brother. Elizabeth, yes, that was it. I was the eldest and felt it was my duty to help out, although there were days when I could have killed for a new frock. Everything I wore was always just slightly behind the latest fashion, even with the help of new ribbons or a gift-pair of new gloves. My admirers did often send me things, pheasants, for example, gloves, once an incredible rainbow-coloured silk shawl. When they sent letters without gifts I was always a little disappointed.

("Dear Letitia, do you remember how we walked with our arms around one another when we were young?") I suppose all famous people get letters like that, often from virtual strangers. "Dearest Letitia, I have woven you a special bookmark depicting a scene from Ethel Churchill," some ghastly scrap that she probably spent hours stitching. Or even worse, "Dear L.E.L., or may I call you Miss Landon? I have taken the liberty of enclosing a small selection of my verse ..."

They want a reply, those versifiers. "Dear Miss X, how kind you were to send me 'A Sonnet Sequence on the Death of my Canary'..." They are hoping you will help them get published, of course, although they never come straight out and say so. I think I can safely state that never once, *never once*, did any of these unsolicited missives contain a spark of genius or even of good yeomanlike workmanship. The bookmarks had more craft than all these ballads or sonnet sequences or meditations in a graveyard. Can't they tell? Ah well, we are told that love is blind and no doubt they love these things they write. If I am feeling kindly, then I do admire their courage, for it takes just as long to write a bad poem as a good one, perhaps longer, and even those of us who have been fortunate enough to have published and been praised, still tremble that next time, next time, we may be laughed at or even reviled. A horse at a mill has an easier life than an author.

And I knew my work would not be fashionable forever, for tastes in art change just as tastes in costume do. I remember going to Madame Tussaud's Waxworks with dear Lady Blessington and she said to me, "One day your likeness will be on display," and I replied, "Complete with my little attic room and my hoard of candle ends?" We laughed, but that night I had a terrible dream about my wax doppelgänger and a great fire in the waxworks. I saw my face melting, my dress on fire, my lips running down my chin and onto my bodice. All the others were melting, too, the kings and queens, the murderers and heroes and soon we all ran together. When the firemen arrived with their water, we had congealed into a great, many-coloured lump full of glass eyes. I woke up with the Misses Lance pounding on my door, asking if I was all right.

I had been reading *Macbeth* and I suppose I was thinking of "Out out, brief candle." Who knows what ideas and images our sleeping selves can yoke together?

I have come a long way from talking about spinsterhood, but from my thirtieth year on, however gaily I presented myself to Society, my future as a single, aged woman was always there in the back of my mind. ("Do offer Auntie the last crumpet." And Auntie, with butter dripping down her whiskery chin and death spots on the backs of her hands, gives a grateful little mew.)

In October 1836, I was staying with Matthew Forster and his family for a few days while my room at the Misses Lance was undergoing a good turnout and a new carpet was laid. My feet had been very cold the winter before, in spite of worsted stockings knitted by Miss Agatha and warm slippers donated by Miss Kate. My little coal fire did not cast the heat very far and as I had never been able to write on my lap, my poor appendages shivered beneath my desk. I often wrote far into the night, indeed sometimes until I heard the milk pails clatter and the sound of horses' hooves in the street below. The solution, or at least a partial solution, was to have a carpet fitted. I decided I could not stand all the fuss this would entail so, leaving the Misses Lance to supervise, I threw myself on the mercy of the Forsters.

When I came down to breakfast on the second morning of my stay (I dislike breakfast, but when one is a guest it is only good manners to put in an appearance, nibble on some toast and try not to look at the gentlemen eating kidneys and sausages, cold beef and pickle), Matthew waved a sheaf of papers at me and said, "This should interest you, Letty!"

"Why would some dull report interest me?" I said, settling myself near the toast rack and marmalade.

"This is not dull; in fact, it's exceedingly interesting, a record of an excursion to Apollonia, on the Gold Coast, where the writer faced down an insurrection by the paramount chief. Quite a feat. And he signed a treaty with the old scoundrel as well."

"That's nice," I said, not terribly impressed.

"And the writer, who is governor of Cape Coast Castle, is on leave here and coming tonight to dine."

"And what is this paragon like?"

"George? An excellent chap, one of our best. Of course *you* want to know if he's handsome."

"That's nonsense. I am much more interested in character than physiognomy."

"Then you must be the exception. In any event, you shall make up your own mind about him."

I took the report up to my room and read it carefully. There were words in it which set my blood racing: *danger; price on my head; stood firm; the royal umbrellas; the heat; success; Africa.* This last made me shiver with excitement. Our hero's full name was George Maclean and so I sent the maid over to Regent Street for a length of Maclean tartan. By teatime I had concocted a shawl, a sash, and even a bit of ribbon for my hair. It was not that I expected much in the way of looks — or even manners. I had seen some of these Old Coasters at Matthew's house before: stringy men, yellowish around the eyeball, prematurely grey or white, hands a bit shaky from the remains of fever or a steady diet of drink. After I became acquainted with cockroaches out there, I had a fancy, because of the similarity of skin colouring, that these ubiquitous insects were nothing but the souls of Old Coasters.

I sat on a chair, in all my Scottish finery, and waited impatiently for George Maclean. Chatted to many of the guests — I was known for my quick wit and merry laugh — but kept an eye out for the hero of Apollonia. I must admit the idea of an Englishman getting the better of a black man out in Western Africa did not seem much of an accomplishment, but Matthew assured me it was, so I had practised looking impressed and intent in front of my looking-glass for a good half hour.

George

I ALMOST DIDN'T GO TO FORSTER'S THAT NIGHT, for I was still recovering from a bad bout of fever and would have preferred dining alone. However, Matthew Forster was chairman of the Committee and I knew he was counting on my being there. Other members had been invited "and they will be most interested to hear how things are going along out there." I knew that most of them really didn't care so long as they made money. The abolition of the slave trade in '33 had hit them in their purses and they were anxious that other trade goods should be found. Gold, palm oil, ivory from the north: none of these added up to the enormous profits of the slave trade. Of course we on the coast were not supposed to traffic in slaves and I never did, but I was an exception. It is not that I had ever been an active abolitionist, but somehow, putting a price on a human being — of whatever colour — bothered me. I arrived at the end of it, when the writing was on the wall and there was a desperation about the business — get as many niggers as you can before the curtain comes down. It was pretty nasty and some trading still went on, in spite of our patrol boats trying to apprehend the slave ships as they left. Not many were caught; those old captains knew all the bays and coves along the coast like the back of their sunburnt hands.

The drawing-room was full of people by the time I arrived, but Matthew must have been looking out for me, for I was barely in the door before he greeted me, grabbed my arm, and said, "There's someone I want you to meet." Through the crush around her I had a glimpse of dark hair, a tartan ribbon, and a bit of tartan shawl. I assumed this was some long-lost cousin of mine that Matthew had dug up.

Letty

"LETITIA," MATTHEW SAID, "I would like you to meet George Maclean, the governor of Cape Coast Castle. George, this is Letitia Landon."

Letty: IF MY FEET HAD NOT BEEN so cold the winter before …

George: If I hadn't felt obligated to turn up that night …

George/Letty: We might never have met.

Letty: What I saw was an auburn-haired man of about my age, with the high colour that goes with the hair, rather full lips, and a very straight back. He looked uncomfortable; he looked as though he would rather be anywhere else.

George: What I saw was a young woman (she looked and dressed much younger than she really was) with pretty dark eyes (slightly protruding), pale, almost translucent skin, and a lively expression. No one could have called her a beauty, but there was something very attractive about her; a sort of intelligent interest in the world seemed to shine forth from her very being.

George

"Are you a Maclean?" I asked.

"Oh, no, no. I have decorated myself like this in your honour."

"Pardon?"

She patted the empty chair next to her.

"Come sit down, please do, so that I don't get a crick in my neck from looking up at you. I have been reading your report of the Apollonia affair and I must tell you how much I admire you."

She held up her hand. Both her hands and her feet were very small, almost child-like.

"Now don't say 'It was nothing!'"

"I would never say that; it was a very difficult situation."

"And did you really have a price of twenty thousand ounces of gold on your head?"

"I did."

"Yet no one took the old king up on this rather splendid offer?"

"No one."

"Weren't you frightened? Might not someone have murdered you — now they do that don't they, out there — then chopped you up and boiled you in a big, black pot?"

He had nice straight teeth when he smiled.

"They are not cannibals, on the Coast, but certainly someone could have shot me or garotted me or done something nasty. That was a lot of money."

"You must be very powerful."

"I think I was very lucky. But also, I didn't back down. They admire that, out there."

Letty: Just then the dinner gong rang and we all went in. Although I was seated next to him, George barely said two words to me or anyone else. And after dinner, he left.

23

George: Jammed up against two strange women and drowning in the scent of eau de cologne, I thought I might faint from embarrassment, truly, I did. I had no store of small talk into which I could dip and so I just kept my head down and ate the excellent oyster soup, the excellent sole, the excellent beef, and so on down the line. The sweet was some icy thing, which called forth oohs and aahs, although I preferred good old-fashioned puddings.

When the ladies withdrew, I made my excuses to Matthew and left, walking back to my hotel in order to clear my head. It never occurred to me that I might see Letitia again. She had told me at one point that she was a writer and I expressed a polite interest, although I could just imagine the sort of romantic nonsense she wrote.

Letty

I WAS QUITE MOVED THAT HE HAD NEVER heard of me. That also meant that he had never encountered any of the malicious whispers that were spread around London from time to time. He did not look like the sort of man who would find such rumours amusing.

And now he had left early, when I was so hoping he would sit by me when we all congregated once again in the drawing room. Matthew said George was recovering from fever and his headache had returned; that is why he left early.

I bit my lip in frustration. Here was this nice man, a nice brave man, who commanded a castle on the Guinea coast, a suitable man, an attractive man (if a bit too serious), a *single* man ("Is your wife here in England with you?" "I do not have a wife") and he had just walked away!

Well, thought I, *in for a penny, in for a pound*. I knew he was staying at The Albany, so the next morning I sent round a small volume of my poetry with a note:

> Dear Mr. Maclean. I send this as a little token of my admiration. Perhaps there are other kinds of courage besides physical? The courage to bare one's soul to the whole world, for instance.
>
> If you are remaining in town for a few days — Matthew tells me that your ultimate destination is your family home in Scotland — would you care to take a dish of tea with me on Thursday, around four? I will be back at No. 22 Hans Place by then and should be delighted to see you. Letitia Landon.

Matthew said, "Well, what did you think of him?"

"Who?"

"George Maclean, of course."

"He seemed pleasant enough. A bit out of his element perhaps."

"I think he's a cut above most of those fellows who make a career out there. I'd trust him with anything."

That night, as I sat brushing out my hair, I said a little prayer — oh please, oh please, oh please. It really was as though he had been sent to me and now I must make sure he didn't get away. I would have to work hard, the way my father used to "work" a salmon trout when he took his annual fishing trip with his cronies. Taking the bait was only the beginning of it, he told me. You had to play the fish, let out a bit of line, then reel it in, let out a bit, until the beast grew tired. Then, and only then, did you bring him in close and net him. One of the few times I broke down, after my father's death, was when I came across his rods and his wickerware creel in the back passage. That, and his spectacles, which he used only for reading the newspaper. My mother wept and carried on for weeks, but then she was of Welsh extraction.

I went to Fortnum's for good, thick-cut marmalade and Scotch short-bread. Ellen, the Misses Lances' maid, put too much sugar in her marmalade, "to take away the bitterness, like." When I attempted to tell her the whole point of using Seville oranges was because they gave such a nice "tang" to the jam, she just gave me a "sniff" — her sniffs were famous in that household — said "yes, Miss Landon," and ignored the advice. I sponged my most demure frock and cleaned my prettiest kid slippers with soft bread. Behind all this activity, which made me abandon writing for a few days, was the terror of being a burden. All the young Oxford and Cambridge men, who flattered me and brought me nosegays, Lord This or Earl That, would never marry such as I. A woman, to marry them, must have Money or Name, preferably both.

George: I must have been mad. When I received her little parcel and the invitation to tea, I was tempted to just ignore it, or at least (it wouldn't be good manners not to reply) send round a note saying I was so tied up with business I must regretfully, etc. etc. I was never sure why I did go; Letty hadn't made such a great impression on me. She seemed a bit of a coquette, almost like an ingenue in a play, but she had read my report, had taken it seriously, and in the half hour before the dinner gong (some fellow Matthew did business with had brought it back from India and he liked to show it off) she asked intelligent questions. And maybe I was a bit lonely; yes, I'll admit to that.

Letty: Flattery and thick-cut marmalade. By four o'clock on a late October afternoon, it was coming on dark and so I could legitimately direct Ellen to draw the curtains in the parlour, make up the fire, and light the lamps. What George saw, when he arrived, was a scene of warmth and domesticity.

"I'm afraid I can't stay long," he said, but of course he stayed and stayed.

George: The teacups were so fragile that I was almost terrified to pick one up. She said they were a present from her late grandmother. I felt like a clumsy oaf in that room, all the little knickknacks on tables, antimacassars on the chairs. Again I was reminded of some play I had seen years ago on leave.

"Are you too warm, Mr. Maclean? I can always ask the maid to open a window."

"Not at all. After one has been on the Coast for several years, coming to England seems like coming to the Arctic. We spend a great deal of our time here shivering."

"And Matthew said you have been ill as well."

"Just the usual, a bad bout of fever. Everyone goes through it. If you survive the first round, you'll usually survive the next — and the next and the next. It's a most insalubrious climate."

"Then why do you stay?"

"I'm not sure, really. Africa will probably be the death of me in the end. I suppose I stay because I'm used to it, and because I'm good at what I do."

Letty: How pretty his hair was in the lamplight. He looked down at the tea tray between us and said, "Good Heavens, did I eat all that?"

"I'm so glad you have an appetite and Ellen will be delighted. Her scones are famous." (Famous for their rocky quality; I bought the scones as well. At least I didn't pretend that I had made them.)

Letty

"Now you must tell me all about yourself," I said. "I know from Matthew you are from the eastern Highlands, but how did you get from there to Western Africa?"

"It's a rather long story," he said.

"We have plenty of time."

And so began our courtship. By the time he finally went up to Scotland we were engaged. Informally engaged, with no one to know but ourselves. This was my idea, on the principle of letting the line out a bit now that I felt he was truly hooked. I said that I wanted to be convinced that *he* was sure before we told the world. Once in Scotland he might change his mind.

"No," he said, "the only thing that worries me is that I'm not sure you really know what you are getting into. The Castle is not like the castles in your childhood fairytales, and the climate really is deadly. I'm not sure I'm doing right by you to encourage you in this. And you will be the only European lady there, except for the missionary wives; the Wesleyans have begun a regular push toward converting the natives to Christianity. We've had missionaries before and certainly services at the Castle, but this is new. Perhaps you can get involved with them?

I doubted that very much, but I just smiled and reminded him that I would have my work. Married or not, my writing would occupy me most of the day.

"Good," he said, "for most of my day will be occupied as well."

When a second week went by with no letter from George, I began to worry. Had I been foolish to suggest we keep our engagement a secret, had I, instead of reeling him in, let him off the hook altogether? I told myself that perhaps he was not a letter-writer, some men aren't, but just a note about the weather, or the journey up, was that so hard to do?

A month went by; my anxiety caused an attack of my old trouble and soon I took to my bed. The hero of Apollonia was not an honourable man. Since all was secret between us, I felt I couldn't ask Matthew Forster if he had heard anything from the Highlands. Matthew was a tease; it would be too risky.

Finally I wrote to Whittington. After all, surely a brother should support his sister in this crisis? He agreed to write to George and ask what his intentions were.

Shortly after that we were engaged again.

My favourite book when I was a child was *Robinson Crusoe*. How I admired that man; how clever he was, how brave! I thought it would be great fun to be shipwrecked on a desert island and have to create everything from scratch. I'd have a Friday, of course — a female Friday, seeing as how I was a girl. She would be big and black and strong, very good at chopping wood and doing manual labour. Even as a young girl I knew I was never cut out for manual labour. My hands and feet were meant to be pretty appendages. My ears were the important thing; my ears and my imagination.

My father had been out to Jamaica when he was a young man. I think he hoped for a career in the Royal Navy, but then the uncle who would sponsor him died — or perhaps there was some quarrel — and I think there was a part of him that bitterly regretted it. He was a romantic, and I was my father's daughter. There was a chief difference, however. He was no good with managing money and I was the opposite. And I had a marketable talent, which was just as well considering his premature death. I don't *blame* him for dying — how could I? — but it made my life difficult. One shouldn't have to write with one eye always on the purse. My brother needed an education; my mother needed help in the care of my sickly sister. There was no one but me, the eldest, to guarantee all this; my uncle did what he could, but he was a curate with a large family — all daughters — and he lived way up in the back of beyond, in Yorkshire.

When I wrote to my mother to tell her that George and I were married ("Captain George Maclean, governor of Cape Coast Castle on the Guinea Coast, a fine man from a good family") she replied almost at once to say she supposed that would be the end of her subsidy. I was so angry that I almost cut her off, but in the end I couldn't do it. I never felt that Whittington or my mother were aware of how hard I worked to provide them with their extra money. I never felt any real gratitude from either of them. I suspect, like the rest of the world, they thought I just "tossed off" a poem here or a novel there in between going to dinner parties and soirées. Even some of my so-called friends said, "You're so prolific, Letty," and I was, but writing is drudgery, writing is *hard work*. There were times when my hand seized up with cramp and had to be massaged with creams before I could take up my pen again, and there were nights when my back ached and my head ached and my eyes felt full of grit. And always there was my old trouble, which sometimes kept me in bed for days at a time.

I had been engaged to a fine man, although he and his crowd denied it later on. I broke it off because of malicious gossip about me and another gentleman.

After that I was so ill I truly thought I was going to die. If it hadn't been for Dr. Thompson and his ministrations I might have slit my wrists just to stop the agony. It is not that I was born sickly, like my sister; in fact I had a good constitution except for this one thing. My "Achilles heel" if you like, only a little farther up.

(And in the evening I was supposed to change from drudge to dazzler, call for the maid to help me with my hair and fastenings. Ellen was a maid-of-all-work, as well as cook, but all-work did not include helping me with my toilette. I was maid as well as Mademoiselle, who struggled with buttons and bows, then pinched my cheeks to make them glow.)

George

I DIDN'T WOO HER; if anything, it was the other way around. Although Africa came into it — oh yes — and the uniform. If I had been a gentleman farmer or a man of business (a man of non-literary business; publishers were a separate breed) I doubt if she would have given me a second look. In her eyes I was a romantic figure. Damned Forster had given her that Apollonia report before she even met me; it was almost as though she conjured me up from that, a different George Maclean from who I really was. Not that I ever pretended to her, never that.

What was I thinking of? She was the last person I should have married — a city woman with city tastes. How on earth would she manage at Cape Coast? And yet, as we walked along together and she took my arm, I felt comforted by her presence. How long had it been since a woman had taken my arm, had pressed my hand, had said, "Tell me all about yourself." You don't think you're lonely out there — or you try to convince yourself that you're not. But you drink too much or you take a country wife, but that only helps with the carnal side of one's nature. Even if you speak the language well (which I did) you can't discuss ideas with such a woman. It's not that I wasn't grateful to Ekosua — she was a wonderful nurse when I was ill, bathing my face with lime juice and water, forcing me to drink some horrible concoction which almost instantly brought relief. And the carnal side — well, that was good too. Young girls mature early out there and I've been told that the old women, at the appropriate time, take them aside and teach them how to please a man. Can you imagine such a thing happening in England?

I was sorry to send her away — Ekosua — but I knew she would understand. I made sure she was given a generous gift of money. William Topp took care of it for me — or at least I hoped he had. I left the ship in the middle of the night, and went in by canoe just to make sure. I told Letty the next day that I had wanted our apartments fumigated with charcoal and thoroughly swept before she set foot in the Castle. I don't think she believed me, but she said nothing. (She knew about my "wife" out here — rumours had reached England — but she seemed satisfied when I said that had been over long ago. Not quite the truth, but a necessary half-truth, for the sake of peace.)

Letty wore just a hint of some eau de cologne she had brought back from a holiday in Paris; she used it sparingly but it was always there and when I at last set off for Scotland in the new year she gave me a small handkerchief dabbed with cologne, "to remind you always of your admirer who awaits your return." I regret to say I left it at the hotel.

Once up at Urquhart I honestly wondered if I hadn't been bewitched by her, her white hands, her dainty feet, her silky hair, the way she said my name — "George," in such an intimate way. It is hard to explain, but to a chap who has spent most of his adult life looking at half-naked women, however lovely (and the young women are truly beautiful), there is something exciting about a woman fully clothed. One can't help thinking about what's underneath all those skirts and petticoats. And the women know it; hence the *décolletage*, if that is the right word, the glimpse of plump shoulders or an ivory neck.

(There were rumours about Letty, hints of a scandal, but I firmly dismissed all this as just talk, envious talk, because she was admired and successful. In any event, I was in no position to cast stones.)

The farther north I travelled, the better I could breathe, and once I left Edinburgh, only stopping for a few hours, I lowered the window on the coach, much to the objections of a stern, black-clad couple, who were my only companions for the rest of the journey — or as far as Aberdeen. They shrank from the fresh air as though it were a poisonous effluvia.

"Just for a moment," I said, with my best smile. "I haven't been home in so long."

If you have never smelled the Highland air, I don't know how to describe it to you. If you have spent your entire life in cities, you might be horrified when I said it smelled of coolness, of heather and peat, of the earth and simple things. (Letty's handkerchief had no place there.) I gulped it, head hanging out, like a schoolboy or a dog.

"If you please, Sir," said the stern, black-clad gentleman.

The dogs recognized me first and set up quite a din. Dusk was falling fast, but there was my father at the door of the manse, holding up a lantern.

"George. You've come at last."

I wondered if I was as much a shock to him as he was to me. How could he have aged so quickly since my last visit — his hair a white cloud around his head, his hands that clasped mine so thin. But his smile was just as warm and the fire burned just as brightly in the parlour. He banished the dogs to the kitchen, where they whined and scratched at the door until he relented — "just this once, mind," he said, although somehow I doubted it was "just this once." The smell of them almost made me weep.

My mother died when I was fourteen and shortly thereafter I joined the army. Since then, I had only been back for short intervals and I did not grow up at Urquhart, but in Keith and then, as a schoolboy, in Elgin, where I boarded with the Latin master. So Urquhart wasn't really "home," in any historical sense, but Scotland was home and my father was home and a Scottish manse is a Scottish manse; this one had the same air of cheerful frugality as the one where I had spent my earliest years. A little bigger, maybe, with a nice glebe surrounding it, but much the same.

My mother's name was Elisabeth and my father had remarried another Elisabeth; it was easy to see that the marriage suited them both. I noticed right away the glances she gave him. Once, after returning to the room with the tea tray ("We'll just have a wee cup the noo, to take the chill off you and supper later.") She set everything down on a low table, then stood up again, and touched him lightly on the shoulder. His hand went up and clasped hers. Would Letty and I have anything like this?

My brother Hugh was a surgeon with the Indian Army, due home on leave in '38 and my other brother, John, my confidante, the brother

I felt closest to, was dead; but my father and stepmother had a son, my half-brother James, who came crashing in about an hour later. He looked like a noisier, more self-confident me at that age, the same wavy red hair, the same rather stocky body. I had not seen him for three years, and he was still a sweet little boy, a "douce laddie" as they would say. He stared at me and I wondered if he were seeing the likeness in reverse ("Is this what I will look like when I am thirty-something?"). He was full of good health and high spirits.

"How do you do, brother George," he said, extending a hand that was none too clean. I took it anyway.

"I've been out hunting," he said.

"And were you successful?"

"Two grouse, which I've left in the larder. I didn't take the old dogs," he explained, "but went alone. They make too much noise. I really need a young dog, Father, and I've seen some nice pups in the town."

"And who will take care of the young dog when you set out on your adventures?"

He smiled at us. I could see what a charmer he was.

"Perhaps he will come with me."

"A variation of Dick Whittington and his cat, perhaps?"

I had a sister who died at twenty-one and my two remaining sisters had married. One was in Elgin and the other in Edinburgh; I had nieces and a nephew I'd never seen. I wondered if James was lonely at all, but it turned out that he, too, had been at Elgin Academy and his final term would start in a few days.

I soon fell into a pleasant routine and tried to forget about Letty; I knew I would have to get out of this engagement, but I wasn't quite sure how to do so. For the first few weeks I deliberately ignored the letters she sent, said nothing to my family (I knew my father would wait for me to speak), and spent most of my daylight hours out of doors.

Letty

WHEN HE WAS VERY ILL just after we landed, he called out a name in his delirium, at least I thought it was a name. "George," I said, "you were calling out last night and the night before: 'Ekosua! Ekosua!' What does that mean? Is Ekosua a name?"

"No, not at all. It's a local curse word."

I didn't believe him so I asked Brodie. "Is Ekosua a name?"

"Why do you ask?" He looked quite uncomfortable.

"Oh, I don't know. I've heard it, more than once; I wasn't quite sure whether it was a name or a command, or what."

"It's a name, a female name. If you were born on a Monday then one of your names will be Ekosua. A boy would be Quashie."

"Hmmm. So did Robinson Crusoe call his Negro servant Friday because that was the day of the week on which he was discovered, or did Friday tell him his name was 'Friday'?"

"He would have said 'Kofi' or some variant of Kofi, if the island was near Africa, but I don't think it was."

"I have a copy with me; I'll look it up. It was my favourite book when I was a child."

"And mine as well."

And so we chatted on and I diverted him from my enquiry about the name Ekosua. George's country wife, Ekosua — Monday's child.

Weeks went by and he didn't answer my letters. Sometimes I felt as though I had conjured him up and then "poof," my phantom lover disappeared. I wrote and wrote to him, nearly every day now. George was a gentleman and a gentleman did not behave in this fashion. (A little voice said "Letty, you let him get away.") Finally I wrote to Whittington. I was terrified the scandalous rumours about me had reached George even up there in the Highlands. No one knew, of course, about our engagement, so there would be no _public_ humiliation, but I would know and that knowledge would kill me. I confided in my closest friend, I had to. I told her I would kill myself if this marriage didn't come off and I meant it. I knew Maria would tell someone in confidence who would tell someone else in confidence and so it would travel through London. Another broken engagement. "Poor Letty," said with a smile and a simper. "Or maybe she made the whole thing up?"

George

IT WAS WRONG OF ME TO KEEP SILENT FOR SO LONG, BUT I DIDN'T know what to do. Finally I asked my father and Elisabeth for advice. The whole sorry tale came tumbling out, how it must have been a *coup de foudre*, how I was an absolute nincompoop when it came to women, how she was the last person I should take out to the Coast; she'd be dead within a month.

"Have you told her that?"

"Not in such harsh words, but yes. The men die like flies, and I understand from a letter from William Topp, who is acting president while I'm away, that of the first group of missionaries who arrived in January, only one remains. The missionaries who already resided there were dead before the others stepped on shore."

"But you knew about the climate when you asked her to marry you."

"I did, I did. And I told her about the snakes and the poison berries, everything I could think of."

"And what did she say?"

"She said, 'You can't scare me.' This is a woman who lives life in her head; she has no idea … In fact, I think she finds all this 'exotic.'"

I put my head in my hands. "What am I to do?"

Elisabeth said softly, "Do you love this woman, George?"

"I thought perhaps I did. Maybe I was simply in love with the idea of having an intelligent companion … out there."

"Does she love you?"

"In her own way, I suppose. We haven't used the word 'love' very much."

"Well," said my father, "you must make your own decision. The lady herself has given you an out. She sent you up here to 'think it over,' before the engagement was made public. You seem to have thought it over and you do not wish to marry."

I could not bear to tell them that her latest letter threatened suicide.

I was not a man who took kindly to threats. I told myself that she was merely hysterical — and justly so, considering my long silence — but suppose she meant it? What then? How could I live with myself?

The day after my talk with my parents, I determined to take a long walk to clear my head and then, that evening, to write to Letty and to tell her in the kindest way possible, that the engagement was off. "My dear sweet Letitia," I would begin, "There is no nice way of saying this ..."

I hiked to Lossiemouth, taking some bread and cheese and a flask of tea with me, and ate my simple meal leaning against a rock and staring out over the soft brown sand at the ocean beyond. The fishermen here were a hardy lot, but their wives were even hardier, hiking up their skirts and carrying their husbands on their backs, out to the boats, so that their garments would not be wet when they set out on those chill waters. When the men returned with the catch, it was these same women who filleted the fish and smoked them and packed them for transport south. All this as well as their ordinary household duties — meals, children, washing, and so on. They might have been ignorant of anything except their own rather narrow world, but even as a boy I admired them (although their children ran after me hurling stones and insults). What a contrast between these women, with their huge, competent hands and wind-scoured cheeks and the hot-house bloom I had asked to marry me. Strange to think that what I was staring at as I ate the last crumbs of cheese was that same ocean I look out on from Cape Coast Castle. So cold here it could drown a man, in wintertime, in a matter of minutes; so warm over there, it felt like soup.

"My dear sweet Letitia," I practised, "I admire you so much, but I cannot find it I my heart to marry you."

"Dear Letty, you told me to go away and think about our engagement, to be 'absolutely sure' — those were your words — that we were right for one another—"

"Dear Miss Landon ..." No, too cold and uncaring.

I sat there most of the afternoon, dreading what was to come, cursing myself for ever getting involved with that woman, but knowing I had waited an unconscionable length of time before writing.

And then there, on the hall table, was a letter from her brother, accusing me of dishonourable behaviour toward his sister, of saying that I had made her ill by my silence, implying, in fact, that I was the cad to end all cads.

No one could be allowed to attack my honour. I could fight a duel or I could marry her. There really wasn't any choice.

I sent off a letter to Letty, apologizing for the long silence, saying I was still terribly worried about her health in that climate, but that if she was game, then so was I.

Letty

"WHAT WILL YOU DO WITHOUT FRIENDS to talk to?" they said.

"Oh," I said, "I shall talk to my friends through my books."

I was about to undertake something new — a series of essays on Sir Walter Scott's women, beginning with Effie and Jeanie Deans in *The Heart of Midlothian*. Scott had said their story was based on a true tale, where a young woman was accused of infanticide.

I was also contracted to do some verse illustrations for a new album. I was a dab hand at that sort of thing. If someone handed me an etching of the Fountain of Trevi, I could produce a suitable poem, with just a touch of melancholy, in spite of never having seen the actual thing. Ditto "A Moroccan Maiden" or "A Tuareg and his Camel."

"Clothed in his robes of brilliant blue —" et cetera, et cetera, et cetera.

I got my wedding without the delights of a wedding. George had said he wanted a quiet ceremony, with no fuss and he preferred we keep our marriage a secret until just before we set sail for the Gold Coast. And so five of us huddled at the front of the church (St. Mary's, in Bryanston Square) one morning in early June and my brother Whittington did his best to make it a solemn occasion, enunciating every word in his beautiful, deep, clergyman's voice.

"Do you, Letitia Elizabeth," "Do you, George Edward," take this man, take this woman. I was a proper Quakeress in my demure gown of dove grey peau de soie, but George looked splendid in scarlet. I felt like the female bird must feel, eyeing her mate's more extravagant plumage. The night before I had a crazy vision of William Jerdan rushing in at the last minute, crying, "This wedding must not go forward" and then recounting our shabby past. A somewhat meagre wedding-breakfast followed and I thanked Heaven for Bulwer's present of some splendid champagne. He made a nice toast, partly in jest, to the "voyage" upon which we were embarking.

George had said he could manage a few days' honeymoon before he went back to his meetings with the Committee. "Fine," I replied, "I always maintained that if I were ever to marry I hoped the honeymoon trip would extend no farther than Hyde Park Corner."

"Oh I think we can stand something a little better than that."

"Paris?"

In the end we went to Eastbourne, to a hotel which had seen better days. No one would know us in Eastbourne. The landlady, too, was in the initial stages of genteel decay: Mrs. Daisy Harkness, a widow. George liked it — lazy walks along the shingle, tramps up the Downs and down the Downs, damp bedsheets in spite of the stone hot-water bottles. A weekend at Browns' would have suited me better. Servants with white gloves, starched linen in the dining-room, silver chafing dishes. As I have said, it's not that I care for breakfast — I rarely partake myself — but the idea of breakfast at a first-class London hotel: that, I like. Coming in with George, my arm tucked into his, the other breakfasters looking up — who is that handsome couple? My goodness, it's L.E.L. There has been a rumour she was married; so *that's* the handsome husband.

My travelling costume, my trousseau, all wasted on the patrons of the Seacliffe Hotel. I could have worn clothes from ten years before. Yet I more and more thought how lucky I was to have found George; it was worth all that tartan material at five shillings a yard and two pairs of good shoes utterly ruined from promenading in the parks and gardens.

We met a dreadful couple at that hotel in Eastbourne. He was some sort of retired officer from Wydah with a thin, sallow wife; he very reddish, she very yellowish; he very stout, she very thin, like Jack Spratt and his wife. They both tied for the first prize in boredom. *Will George be like that, when he's old?* I thought. *Even more terrifying, will I be like her?*

Of course she had to warn me about the "terrible dangers" of life in Africa.

"Do you mean the snakes? The driver ants? The diseases?"

"I mean, Mrs. Maclean, the servants. You can't trust any of 'em. They'll slit your throat if they get worked up with palm wine or rum and think you've done 'em an injury. Keep everything locked up — everything. Be severe. Threaten flogging." She leaned even closer. "Don't ever let them touch you!

"You see, what you will shortly discover is that these creatures have no moral sense, none whatsoever. And as for their customs, their beastliness. Dis-gus-ting," she said, enunciating every syllable.

"Do you have no happy memories?"

"Ha. Not really. Charles does, many. But it's different for men. Women have to be always vigilant, always on guard. And should you be—" her voice dropped to a whisper "— *violated* in your dressing-room while your husband is on trek, do you think other black servants will come to your rescue? Not likely."

I thanked her for her advice and excused myself. She called after me, "Flannel next to the skin!"

George stayed down for at least another hour.

"Awful old bore," he said.

"Why, then, did you linger?"

"Oh well, he wanted to talk. I think he misses all the fun."

"The fun?"

"Yes."

I was already in bed, under the damp sheets and damp eiderdown.

"Come to bed, George, before I freeze to death."

He blew out the lamp and whispered, "Dear Letty, I shall be gentle."

(I had contemplated making a small cut on my wrist and collecting the blood in a tiny vial, so that there would be "proof" of my chastity. I gave up the plan because I didn't think George was the sort to notice such things.)

There were a few strokings, a few thrusts, a few little whimpers from me, and then we were truly One.

Just before he turned over and fell asleep, he said, "What was the wife going on about?"

"About how much fun it was going to be. In Africa."

We went back up to London after three days and stayed with friends until we left for the ship. Our marriage had been found out, probably through Bulwer, who could never keep a secret, and I did get some of the attention and presents a bride is entitled to. I hardly saw George; he didn't even take time off for Queen Victoria's Coronation procession, but I watched it with great interest, surrounded by friends. We were looking down from a second-storey balcony, to avoid the throngs that lined the streets, so of course we couldn't see her face as the carriage passed, but I couldn't help but wonder what her life would be like, every moment of her day regulated according to tradition. Every movement observed; every utterance noted. I didn't envy her, our first reigning queen since Queen Anne. What is that old proverb? "A favourite has few friends." In my own, much smaller way, I had discovered how true this was. Detractors, scandal mongers — they buzzed around me like wasps. Indeed, there was a nasty scandal sheet called exactly that, *The Wasp*.

Would Victoria succeed or fail? She was very young, eighteen, nineteen? And would need good advisers. Even so, how many of those courtiers who bowed to her and fawned over her today, would secretly wish her ill? How well Shakespeare understood all that: "Uneasy lies the head that wears a crown!"

If I had not married George, I would no doubt have lived to what they call a "ripe old age." But in what circumstances? My popularity was already waning, my commissions for scrapbook verses drying up, and prose becoming more and more popular. I could write prose, but only of a certain sort. Mr. Dickens's star would shine brighter and brighter, for he had the ability to combine dead mothers and mistaken identity with a picture of life in England in all its harshness for any but the wealthy. I could "do" faithful old nurses but I couldn't really portray the life of the streets, couldn't really re-create London the way he could. I didn't know enough and perhaps I didn't feel enough. My mother used to accuse me of being cold and self-centred, with no sympathy for my poor afflicted sister. Perhaps it was true; I didn't have time for sympathy. I needed to write and write and write. If I didn't write I should die.

And so, what would I have been like in a few years down the road? Would I be able to find another set of adoring old maids like the Misses Lance when I was an old maid myself? I had visions of scrag ends of beef, cooking for myself, saving candle ends, turning the sheets to make them last, doing my own washing and mending, my fingers rough and unsightly. Of course, if George had died first and I returned to England as a widow, with some sort of pension, that would be different.

And finally — death. A small notice in the *Times*. "Oh," says somebody at a dinner party, "I read today that L.E.L. has died. You know, the poetess. Quite the rage in her day."

Her neighbour at table shakes his head. "The name means nothing to me, I'm afraid. This grouse is excellent." Perhaps it is better, in the long run, to experience sudden death? My story, at least, will live on. Those who walk through the Castle courtyard a hundred years from now will pause at our two graves, side by side, will be told the story.

"But there is still a mystery surrounding her death."

We sailed on the fifth of July, in the brig *Maclean*, travelling down by train as far as we could go, and then on by coach. I had never been on a train before and loved it, in spite of the noise and rocking to and fro, in spite of the grime.

"We must build railroads in Africa!" I said to George. "Such fun."

Whittington was a member of the farewell party; he had insisted on it, although George, for some reason best known to himself, was barely civil to him. George's brother Hugh was with us as well, but as we missed the first train and he did not, we did not join up with him until Portsmouth. Hugh was a surgeon in the Indian Army and home on leave, much more polished in manner than George; quite charming. If I had seen him first perhaps I would have been going out to India instead of darkest Africa. But I didn't.

He had not arrived back in England in time for our wedding or he certainly would have stood up for George. As it was, he docked and then went immediately to Urquhart to pay his respects to his family, sending round a note that he would meet with us before we sailed. You might think it strange that I did not invite my mother. Shouldn't a bride have her mother by her on her "great day"? I told Whittington not to discuss the wedding with her until it was over and he agreed. She would have found fault with everything — my dress made me look sallow, all the secrecy boded ill — "Your husband must have something to hide" — the breakfast was "a poor sort of affair." Things like that. Any praise would be reserved for her son. Having written to assure her that her stipend would continue to be paid through my bank, I felt I had done enough. I have such happy memories of my father — swinging on the gate as I awaited his return from town.

Up on his horse, such a chestnut beauty, he looked down at me from a great height. Later, when I read about Centaurs, that image came to mind, my father on his horse, looking down at me. I loved the way he said, "Well, Letty, how's my girl today?" then dismounted and handed me the reins. I loved the way he smelled — of horse, of tobacco, but also of London, the place I longed to be. Frankly, I was glad when he couldn't keep up the farm; I hated the country even then, and wanted to kiss the cobbles when we returned to civilization.

The next morning George did not come down until nearly noon, so I had a chance to write a few more farewells while Whittington and Hugh took a long walk about the town. I tried to imagine what on earth they would find to talk about, but perhaps they spent the time extolling the virtues of their respective siblings. They seemed quite congenial, at any rate, when they returned.

We ate a cold luncheon and very soon after we were told it was time to go down, the tender was waiting. As we stepped on board the *Maclean* the guns fired a salute that quite startled me and set my ears ringing. All the sailors were lined up to greet Governor Maclean and his wife. And when we went below and I saw the tidy cabin that was put at my disposal, with every possible little luxury provided — soft towels, French soap, a small looking-glass, a table for my travelling writing-desk, a chair, even a vase of fresh flowers, such a charming gesture. I smiled at George. "You have a touch of the romantic after all."

He laughed. "I must confess it was Hugh's idea. I think he has had more to do with ladies than I have." He waved his arm. "It's all right then, is it? You'll be comfortable?"

I nodded and we trooped back up on deck, where, to my surprise, I was introduced to a rather stout woman named Mrs. Bailey. She was the chief steward's wife and was to be my companion for my first few months at the Castle. Her cabin was next to mine and should I want anything I was to knock three times on the wall. George had a small cabin to himself, next to the captain's, as he said he would be spending most of his time on deck or with the officers.

Our trunks and boxes had all been sent down early, so once the cabin baggage had been deposited, we had to say goodbye to our brothers; the captain was anxious to catch the tide. As Whittington stood in the tender, looking up, I threw him down my purse. "There," I called, "look after this for me; I shan't need it where I'm going."

Away they went and then away we went. I stood on deck waving a white handkerchief until I could have been no more than a dot to them. I had been across the Channel to Paris, so I was not unfamiliar with the sight of England receding behind me, but this was different, this was adventure of a very high order.

"Africa," I whispered to myself. "Africa." I felt as though all the events of my life had been leading up to this moment.

George came to fetch me for tea.

"I am so happy," I said to him, linking my arm in his. "I am so very, very happy."

"Come below now, Letty," he said. "Later on, you will put on your heavy cloak and we'll look at the stars together. Nowhere are they more beautiful than when seen from the deck of a ship."

We did that, and then the next day the ship began to roll and my love for the sea disappeared, and with it my determination, as a child, to "marry a pirate and sail the seas." Not only was I dreadfully seasick, the helpful Mrs. Bailey was even worse — no help at all. The sea became so violent that all the furniture was lashed together, the bed to the table, the table to the chair, and the only way I kept from rolling out of my bunk was by placing bolsters on each side of me. I could eat nothing and could drink only small sips of watered wine. There were days when I felt my old self would turn itself inside-out, like a glove. It is really impossible to describe seasickness unless you have experienced such violent upheavals yourself. George looked in from time to time to make sure I wasn't dead, sent broth, or whatever he thought I might fancy.

"What I fancy is being thrown overboard."

"Poor Letty." And off he went, the picture of robust health. I hated him.

After we stopped at Madeira and took on arrowroot and citrus fruits, I began to feel a little better, but I was very weak and the nausea never completely left me. I did go up on deck a few times, after the Bay of Biscay, but I thought to myself that all the various horrors of Cape Coast must be truly horrific indeed, if they could top weeks at sea in the brig *Maclean*.

One night, when the sea was relatively calm and I had managed to keep down some ginger beer and a biscuit, George asked if I would enjoy a short stroll on deck. I felt I should make the effort, for his sake, if not for mine, and so I wrapped myself in a shawl (no need for heavy clothing now) and after a few turns stood at the rail with him. We were not too far off Sierra Leone, where George had been secretary to the governor at one time.

"Nothing is so reassuring, after crossing such a broad expanse of water, as the sight of land. It won't be too long now before those winking lights will be the lights of home."

"Do you think of it as home, George, the Gold Coast?"

"Ach, Scotland will always have a hold on my heart, but it's important to put that behind me when I'm out here. Men who don't, men who can't accept it or adjust to it, can sicken and even die."

I waited for him to say something romantic like, "Home is wherever you are, from now on," but of course he wasn't that sort of person.

Unwilling to quit the beautiful moonlight, which made everything seem as bright and clear as day, we just stood there, listening to the jingle-jangle of the rigging above us, each wrapped in our own thoughts, until I looked down.

"What's that out there?" I pointed to something floating close to the ship. George looked where I was pointing and then swiftly turned me around. "Don't look, Letty. Just return to your cabin."

"But ..."

"Just go."

But I had seen; it was the ghastly, bloated, headless body of a man.

I did as I was told, but could hear shouts and running feet above my quarters. The next day there was no mention of this incident; it was as if it had never happened.

Had that *thing* been black ... or white?

I did manage to write a few poems, one of which, "Ode to the Evening Star," I thought quite fine. Still, I'd rather find my inspiration for poetic subjects while on dry land!

George and I had an arrangement; if, after three years, I had had enough of the Coast, I could return to England. He would come home on leave from time to time and eventually retire. This was a not unpleasant thought. In three years I would have enough anecdote and adventure to dine out whenever I felt like it; my book of essays about Scott's heroines would, hopefully, be published, and all those old scandals would have died down. "L.E.L. is back," the reviews would state, "and her star is brighter than ever!" A garden flat somewhere, or a house, even, filled with curios. An elephant's foot umbrella stand (I saw one of those somewhere) or strange carvings.

Matthew Forster shook his head and said, "Letty, Letty, you'll be back on the next boat that lays off Cape Coast Town."

"Nonsense," I replied. "I may like it so much I'll choose not to come back at all."

We landed on the fourteenth of August, or rather, we stood off, in the roads, for no ship could actually "land" at that spot, the sea so fierce and the rocks so treacherous. There was a thick fog and we could see nothing; it felt as though the whole world were wrapped in thick, wet, white wool. Hot, as well, hot and humid. All we could do, the captain said, was wait until the canoe-men came out in the morning. Meanwhile, we stood on deck, peering through the fog, anxious to be off and away from this hated prison of five and a half weeks and onto dry land. We could hear the crashing of the surf beyond, but we couldn't see it. And there was a strange smell, very faint, like a conservatory or florist's shop, plus something more acrid, which George said would be the charcoal fires in the town.

"This fog is not really healthy, Letty, and you are very new to the climate. I suggest you go below and get to bed early. Tomorrow will be a busy day."

It was hard to sleep, not just from the excitement, but from the sensation that the ship was still rolling violently from side to side. My mind told me it wasn't; my body told me it was. I finally dozed, but was startled awake by the sound of feet tramping above. The next morning I discovered George had decided to disembark — a canoe had come out for him — and arrived at the Castle on his own. I was very surprised at this behaviour and a little put out, but he explained it away later by saying he wanted to be sure the rooms had been adequately aired and fumigated and that everything was ready for my reception. He paid for all this concern for my wellbeing — if that's what it was — by catching a bad chill, which laid him up for days.

George

I HAD TO MAKE SURE THAT WILLIAM TOPP had seen to things. The other wasn't a lie — about our apartments. Letty deserved pleasant, airy, clean rooms upon her arrival. She'd been terribly seasick throughout the voyage and now it was my duty to make her life at the Castle as comfortable as possible. I had to make sure the apartments had been smoked. It was just bad luck that I fell ill — too long in Britain had weakened me. Of course there was the other worrying business as well.

Letty

THE MISTS CLEARED BEFORE NOON and there was the Castle, shining whitely in the sun. George was right; it did not look like the Rhinish castles from my children's books, but it was very impressive just the same. It was only up close that one saw what the climate had done to it — great chunks of whitewashed plaster had fallen off and this gave the walls a scabrous appearance — the whole exterior had to be redone once a year. Everything decayed in the heat and humidity. I had been advised not to bring any books that I really treasured, for mould and worms would soon attack them. A writer, however, cannot live without a few of her favourites, so I had packed one little case with books I felt were absolutely essential and my travelling writing kit contained enough paper, quills, wafers, and quill nibs — such a *good* invention — to keep me going for some time. George said there was no need for me to bring blotting-paper as there was "sand aplenty."

We were lowered into the enormous dugout canoes that came out to fetch us — our goods in one, ourselves in another. Later Mrs. Bailey said she "didn't know where to look without blushing," for the canoemen wore nothing but a small strip of cloth around their loins. I understood for the first time what "girded his loins" really meant. Their torsos were magnificent, brown and gleaming with some sort of oil — like the statues of Greek gods I had seen in books — all muscle and male beauty. I have no aptitude for painting, but I did wish there were someone present who could record this scene in full colour: the dazzle of the sunlight on the water, the strength of the men as they dipped and raised their paddles (which were shaped like wooden tridents), the Castle in the distance, the two European ladies hanging on to their parasols for dear life.

When we were nearly ashore, four giants waded out through the surf and we were placed on their crossed arms, two giants to each lady, and carried to the watergate, where we were set down carefully by Gog and Magog and their brothers. Our skirts were wet at the bottoms, but they would soon dry. I wanted to kneel down and kiss the land ("Oh Land, there were times when I feared I should never see you again; Oh Land, I shall never take you for granted again!") but I felt that might embarrass George. After all, I was now the governor's lady. I did think that I must make time that very afternoon to jot down my first impressions.

George was waiting in the courtyard, all the servants assembled, and the soldiers who looked after the few prisoners. Most of the servants were men, although there were four young girls whom I later discovered were called "pra-pra girls" and were responsible for sweeping the courtyard every day with little hand brooms called pra-pras. They were very pretty, giggled and lowered their eyes when I smiled at them.

My husband escorted me up the broad staircase to our rooms, which were much nicer than I dared to hope. There was one large bed-sitting room for the two of us, then a slightly smaller separate bedroom and boudoir for myself. My rooms were at the seaward side of the Castle, and, as we were fairly high up, they would catch whatever breeze might blow in across the water. All of our private quarters were distempered a pretty pale blue and in our shared areas there were prints upon the walls. I was quite surprised to see that they were copies of Boyden's prints of scenes from Shakespeare's tragedies: *Othello*, *Macbeth*, *Lear*, etc. Everything was extremely tasteful; it was hard to believe that just a few metres away was a town of about six thousand Negroes plus a few merchants and missionaries.

George said, "My secretary died while I was away, so I will have to leave you to your own devices until dinnertime; I expect both you and Mrs. Bailey would like to rest. I'll see that tea and sandwiches are sent up for both of you and we'll meet again around seven."

There was a rather large packing box in the corner. (It said: FRAGILE. It said THIS SIDE UP. It said, FOR MRS. MACLEAN.)

"Would you like me to open it?" George asked.

"Of course I would."

He took a hammer that I hadn't noticed (it was lying on top of the box) and proceeded to carefully dismantle the box, saving each piece of wood, each nail, each strap and piling them neatly in a corner. When it was all done, he stood up and the contents were revealed: a most exquisite escritoire.

"Oh, George. How lovely."

"A belated happy birthday, Letty. I couldn't present it to you until we landed. It even has a secret drawer with a separate key."

I threw my arms around him, which embarrassed him mightily. "We shall have no secrets from one another, so there is no need of such a secret drawer, but I do love the desk and know I shall use it constantly. You have made me so happy."

He left me then; Mrs. Bailey went to her own quarters, which were nearby, and within the half-hour there was a knock on the door and a young voice saying, "Cock, cock, cock."

"Come in," I called, and so entered Isaac, carrying a covered tray. I discovered that he always announced himself, "cock, cock, cock," as well as knocked; this was a great source of amusement to both George and myself. I suppose he was about thirteen years old — he wasn't sure when I asked him — one of the "sense boys" who was training to be a servant, in this case, a cook.

I nibbled on a sandwich, drank a cup of tea, closed the louvres, changed into a loose frock, and fell asleep almost immediately. I did not dream — why would I? Africa was a dream.

That night we dined alone and the next morning George handed me a set of keys and I frankly confess I brought with me a plentiful stock of ignorance.

"Are these for Mrs. Bailey?"

"No, my dear, they are for you. As my wife, you are now the chatelaine of the Castle. I speak only of the domestic side. Everything else is under my supervision."

George

THIS IS WHEN I DISCOVERED Letty had no idea about household management, no idea at all. She had never cooked, never weighed or measured anything, never written out a menu. I suppose, as a son of the manse, where a local girl might come in to help a few times a week, but otherwise all the cooking and all the ordering of supplies was done by my mother, and then my stepmother, I assumed my wife would have some rudimentary domestic skills at the very least. But Letty hadn't lived at home for years; she was always resident in someone else's home, with her Grandmother Bishop, then the Misses Lance, or visiting some friend or other. She had no idea how to go about things and I admit I was exasperated at her ignorance. My wife was a woman who had lived almost entirely in her imagination. I explained what I could and then I introduced her to Ibrahim, my cook of many years, and directed him to instruct her. I could see she wasn't too pleased, but I'll say this for her, she never complained, at least not to me.

Letty

YOU MAY WONDER WHY I NEVER seemed to be afraid in my first few weeks at Cape Coast. It was not as though I had seen many Negroes in London. Some of the great houses had Negro servants — I remember one charming little black boy who carried an enormous fan of white feathers — but they were always in the background. Servants serve, by definition.

Here there were Negroes by the hundreds, ordinary people who led their lives in the town just beyond the Castle or set out in their dugout canoes to fish the surrounding waters.

Even the prisoners who cleaned (always supervised by an armed officer or two) didn't worry me. I was known to have a sensitive, rather nervous nature — why wasn't I afraid?

I've thought about this. I remembered the warnings of that dreadful woman in Eastbourne. She had obviously lived a life of fear out there. I don't really have an answer. Perhaps, from the time I was carried ashore by those two giants, I felt as though I were living in a book, that nothing was quite real. When I woke up that first afternoon I wasn't quite sure where I was and whether what I awoke to was really a dream.

Later on, when things were left outside my door, when someone invisible to me stood there and laughed — then I was afraid. That was different.

Letty

I LEARNED FAST, thanks to Ibrahim and young Isaac. Within a week I could scold with the best of them, give out the appropriate amount of salt, sugar, palm oil, whatever was needed, order dinner, always the same unless we were having guests: two fowl and some yam, fresh fruit. George said he could never get enough of the wonderful fruit out here, since fruit, except for a few berries, was unknown in the eastern Highlands where he grew up. Only once did I forget to lock up the meat safe and Mrs. Bailey — who had taken a shine to Ibrahim and was teaching him to make stodgy puddings, much to George's delight — had gone down to the kitchen to remind the cook to soak some raisins for a Spotted Dick she intended to make and discovered two of the resident soldiers, faces slathered in grease and the carcass of a cold roast turkey under the table, where it had been hastily kicked when they heard her footsteps on the stair. Mrs. Bailey never told on me, I'll say that for her, and it really was I who suffered, for I was to have enjoyed a bit of that turkey with some roast yam for my lunch.

From the time we arose, just before dawn, and shared a morning cup of tea and some arrowroot ("cock cock cock" went Isaac, at the door) until seven in the evening, I rarely saw George. He was used to having his luncheon, which he called "relish" with various merchants and officers in the big mess hall. A long lunch, with far too much alcohol as far I was concerned. I began to understand all those other cases marked FRAGILE, which had come up from the hold of the *Maclean*. Case after case of wine, but also brandy and rum, from which they made a punch with limes and sugar.

George had a prodigious appetite, for even after a heavy luncheon he could still tuck into the evening meal and finish off with a pudding. "Letitia," he said, "it is important to eat in the tropics; you must keep up your strength." He always called me "Letitia" when he wanted to emphasize a point; my father had done the same.

The Castle itself was like some great white ship, the enormous courtyard its deck, the soldiers' quarters, except for their families, might have been the sailors' quarters and "below decks" were the cells where the prisoners were kept: the "hold."

One hundred feet from one end of the courtyard to the other? I never asked, but it certainly seemed that large. I never really explored while I lived there, stuck mainly to our apartments and the dining areas, the battlements which looked out to sea.

Every so often I said to myself, "Letitia, you are living in a real castle — at least it calls itself a castle and that's good enough for you. And my husband, George Maclean, is 'king of the castle,' so I must be the queen."

After playing mistress of the Castle, I hurried to my room and wrote all morning. In the heat of the day I rested or read until it was time for dinner. The rainy season was supposed to be ending, but one afternoon the skies opened and a torrent of rain descended; I had never seen anything like it. It was Biblical, the sort of rain poor Mr. and Mrs. Noah must have experienced as they floated away with their menagerie in the ark. But it was over well before dark and the brief interval of coolness was lovely. These were the "small rains" George said, and soon they would stop altogether; then there would be no rain at all for at least four months and all the lush green would turn to brown.

"If these are the 'small rains,'" I said, "I hate to think what the large rains are like."

He said the people out here, black as well as white, longed for the Dry Season, for it was considered much healthier, with less chance of fever.

"Will I get fever, George, before the Dry Season begins?"

"I hope not, Letty, you are such a tiny thing, but I expect you will."

"This first fever — is this what Matthew called the 'seasoning'?"

"It is."

"This is what the missionaries died of?"

"That, and dysentery."

When we arrived all the little band of Wesleyans who had come ashore the previous January were dead, with one exception, Mr. Thomas Birch Freeman. The officers called the graveyard "The Stone Garden," since its crop of gravestones seemed to flourish year after year after year.

And yet I seemed to thrive. George caught a chill and was laid up for four days just after we disembarked — penance for his midnight dash through the fog — but I caught nothing. Indeed, I had never felt better in my life. The old trouble was there; like the poor, it was always with me, but I had my drops and the ache or pain or whatever it was that plagued me, was manageable.

One afternoon I asked Mr. Freeman how it could be that I, miserable sinner, should be spared, when five of his party had succumbed within the first few weeks of landing on these shores. Surely God must have a wicked sense of humour?

But more of Mr. Freeman in a few minutes. Mr. Freeman is like a character in one of Shakespeare's plays who has little or nothing to do in Act I, but features prominently from then on.

The actual cleaning of the Castle rooms was done by the prisoners, guarded over by a soldier with a bayonet. They took forever to do anything, not that they were stupid, simply lazy. George told me that when two of Captain S's men ran away and were caught, they said they couldn't abide the way the soldiers stood so close to them, they couldn't carry on a private conversation. At any rate, the present lot took all morning to do what a good old English char could accomplish in an hour. Still, I suppose it keeps them out of mischief. They do love "waxin'" day, when the few floors that are made of wood or painted cement are waxed. They strap heavy bricks on their sandals, the bricks covered with a duster, throw down gobbets of floor polish, and glide across the floors like Dutchmen on the canals. The parquet floors are beautiful, but the white ants think so, too, and what looks solid on the surface can be completely eaten away underneath. The floors in all of our apartments, except my bedroom, are paved with marble squares, black and white, like a chessboard, much more durable, but they do show every bit of grime and are slippery directly after mopping.

The town is spread out behind the Castle and that part which is occupied by the poorest classes consists of houses made of swish with palm-leaf roofs. In the parts of the town where Europeans live — the merchants — or wealthy natives, the houses are very different, made of brick, whitewashed, with flat roofs and green shutters. They are really most attractive. The two principal streets are very wide and lined with umbrella trees. The chapel is at one end of the main street, directly facing the Castle.

Beyond the town there is a series of hills, covered with dense brushwood or "bush."

Chickens and children wander freely, women walk to and fro with babies strapped to their backs; men sit under a huge silk-cotton tree, talking and playing a game they call Oware.

I had never seen another woman's breasts until I came to Cape Coast and at first I found it quite shocking, but what shocked me even more was the way the men of both races — except for Mr. Freeman, of course — ignored this nakedness.

Women of childbearing age wear their cloths tucked up under their armpits, but the young and the old leave their bosoms exposed. They wear no supporting undergarments of any kind and the old women's breasts hang down almost to their waists. However, it seems that no one ever mocks these old crones or shows them any disrespect.

There is so much insect life here! Termites chewing away, mosquitoes whining at night, driver ants who can deliver a sting like a wasp, things munching, marching along, relentless armies of minute destroyers. And spiders! Huge spiders. Everything seemed excessive out here and vaguely — or not so vaguely — tinged with malevo-lence. There were only two things I grew fond of: the little geckos that hid behind picture frames waiting for unsuspecting flies, and the orange-tailed lizards that sunned themselves on the battlements and gazed at me with such ancient, knowing eyes. What we have seen, they seemed to say; what tales we could tell. Ibrahim, whose English is quite good, told me that small boys like to grab them by the tails, which the clever creatures divest themselves of immediately and scamper to freedom. Apparently their tails grow back, but never quite as long. I could not but think of Shakespeare's "wanton boys."

George (as he headed off for the day): All right Letty? Any complaints?
　Me: No complaints, Dear.
　George: Right then. See you just before dinner.

George: Why shouldn't I have believed her? Letty was never a person to hide her feelings. If she said things were fine, what reason did I have to assume anything other? If she had been unhappy, I would have been the first to know it.

Letty

ON THE THIRD EVENING, before George came down with fever and chills, and after my brain had stopped trying to convince my body that we were still on the rocking ship, after I could get "a proper night's rest" (his words), we gave a small dinner party so that I could be introduced to the principal merchants, the few officers who weren't dead and Mr. Thomas Birch Freeman, head of the Wesleyan Mission to the Gold Coast.

He picked up my hand, bent low over it as though he were going to kiss it (I saw George's look of astonishment), but merely shook my hand, said, "Mrs. Maclean." His hand was rough as a cat's tongue, his work-hardened, pinkish palm. He didn't say much that evening, although when the bottle went round he put his hand over his glass and laughed — *hee-hee-hee* — saying he preferred "Adam's Ale," thank you.

The dinner was excellent: a fish course, the fish resembling our mullet, then roasted yam and roasted plantain, then a ground-nut stew, something I had never tasted before and quite liked, although it was too spicy. I couldn't believe my eyes when all of the men added more red pepper from little saucers that had been set up and down the long table. As it was, my nether regions suffered the next day, as I was sure they would. Joloff rice. Fresh pineapple spears. Wine and more wine.

They were all very gallant towards me and I enjoyed myself immensely, although I wasn't so naive as to think they weren't sizing me up. I think they expected some sturdy Highland lassie and not this tiny Londoner.

"Do you read poetry, Mr. Hutton?"

"Not if I can help it." But said with a smile. "I'm afraid you'll find us rather a rough lot compared with your friends back in London."

Mr. Freeman: After meeting her, bets were taken on how long she'd last. The general opinion was that she'd be dead within a fortnight. What had Maclean been thinking of? Hard to imagine him as so besotted he'd marry a slip of a woman like this, but then, I barely knew him.

Letty: How wonderful it was to sit at dinner with a group of attentive men, even if they didn't read poetry. Dinner parties bring out the best in me, although I thought if Mr. Freeman said, "Adam's Ale! Adam's Ale" one more time, as the bottle went around, I would scream. I made him pay for that a few days later.

"Tell me, Mr. Freeman, when Adam delved and Eve span, is it possible he was cultivating the grape?" I asked.

"I'm sure he was cultivating all manner of good things."

"Well, we don't know how long it was before the First Couple were banished from the Garden, but suppose there was time for the vines to flourish and Adam to discover the delights of fermentation?"

"And so …?" He didn't quite see where this was going, but I could tell he was uneasy.

"And so, could 'Adam's Ale' have been wine, not water?"

"I am not a Biblical scholar, Mrs. Maclean, just a simple man with a mission. Perhaps that is a question for someone with more knowledge than I possess."

"But suppose you are denying yourself the benefit of alcohol — and is it not generally acknowledged that there *are* benefits — because of a misinterpretation?"

"I would not take alcohol in any case."

"And why is that?"

"I took a pledge."

"I see."

I was wrong to tease him. He was probably the good Christian he presented himself as, but I didn't care for him at all. I tried, because George liked him. Well, to be perfectly honest, I didn't try very hard.

George: You don't like Mr. Freeman, do you?

Me: Not much. He thinks he's an Englishman.

George: He is an Englishman, born and bred in England. The fact that he's a mulatto doesn't make him any less an Englishman.

Me: Haven't you noticed how he says "we," all the time, "We must work hard to educate and save these benighted souls." No sense of fraternity with them at all. He told me that he is "heartbroken" at their ignorance of civilized customs. He seems to look down on the natives from a great height. It bothers me; it reminds me of that dreadful woman in Eastbourne, with all her whispered insinuations.

George: Are you defending the local customs? Have you become an expert in four weeks?

Me: Brodie has been helping me to understand.

George: Ah, Brodie Cruickshank. You're cavalier.

Me: Thus we hear the first mention of the fourth principal actor in this tale. But we have to get back to Mr. Freeman.

Mr. Freeman

MY FATHER WAS A FREED SLAVE who had worked for years at the plantations in Jamaica. I do not know if he came from this area or farther along the Guinea Coast, but he was definitely an African from Africa, snatched when he was a small boy and marched down to the Coast, shackled at the neck, just one in a long line of terrified men, women, and children. He may have been confined here in Cape Coast Castle; I'll never know because he couldn't remember very much from the first part of his journey.

He met my mother in London. She was a widow with three children and housekeeper at a place where he became an under-gardener. I followed my father around as he planted and pruned, so is it any wonder that I, too, became a gardener?

There were so many things I wanted to ask my father, but he was a silent man, almost speechless except when he was talking about plants. He wore his shirt even on the hottest days, but one evening, when I couldn't sleep (my half-brothers always pushed me to the very edge of the bed), I crept downstairs and there was my father with his shirt off and my mother rubbing some kind of unguent into his back. His back was covered in strange welts; they looked like long worms that had burrowed into his body. I later knew what those "worms" really were — the healed-over marks of the lash. I crept back upstairs and neither of them noticed me, but I never forgot the sight of his poor mutilated back in the flickering light. I wanted to rush to him and throw my arms around him, but I knew it would shame him to know that I had seen. For a long time I hated every white man, hated my brothers, even, to a certain extent my mother; but because she loved him and rubbed the marks of his wounds with her special salve, I did not include her in my general hatred.

And she had plans for me, they both did. They had seen my interest in botany and sent me off to study at Kew Gardens. Where they obtained the money for this I do not know. My brothers were resentful and called me names out of earshot of my parents: half-caste; woolly-head; freak. I expect they would have liked to escape the village as well and were jealous of my preferment. They attacked me in ways that would be most hurtful — taunts about the colour of my skin. Children know instinctively how to be cruel: mop-head, nigger-boy. Had he known, my father would have thrashed them within an inch of their lives with my dear mother calmly looking on. When I walked away one sunny morning in October, I knew I was walking away forever.

My father accompanied me for a mile or two and then he stopped and shook my hand. "Good luck, Thomas, you will need it; the wide world can be a harsh and difficult place. We shall pray for you every day." His big black, work-hardened hand seemed reluctant to let mine go. I was fourteen years old, and although my eyes swam with tears and I looked back more than once at the shrinking figure of my father, my natural cheerfulness soon banished the gloom. The birds were singing, the sky was blue, and I was on the way to Richmond and my future.

It wasn't very long before I was a botanist and first under-gardener and then head gardener at Orwell Park, near Ipswich. Sir Robert Harland was most impressed that I could not only read and write with great fluency, but that I knew the Latin name of almost every flower and tree I came across. When Sir Robert and Lady Harland had house parties, they often came out to the gardens to show me off. There was a walled garden, with espaliered fruit trees, a knot garden, glass houses where I grew melons, cucumbers and huge purple grapes. I became a bit of a local celebrity, but I never forgot my parents and visited them two or three times a year, bringing a large basket of produce (with my employers' permission of course). My half-brothers had long gone to seek their fortunes in London and I never saw them again.

I had a good life at Orwell Park. I even acquired a small library of my own, botanical books, mostly, and I hope this does not sound too prideful, but in later years I even corresponded with Sir William Hooke.

I heard from time to time about the abolitionists and I hoped they would win out against the opposition and that no one would ever again have to suffer the way my father and thousands of others had had to suffer, but I did not discuss this with the other servants because I knew Sir Harland was in the other camp. I suppose it did not affect me personally — or so I thought at the time — and therefore my mind did not dwell on the struggle in any meaningful way. (And my father never mentioned it to me; perhaps he was convinced Wilberforce and his supporters would fail.) He did begin to tell me what his life in Jamaica had been like. Slowly, although every word opened up an old wound. "I want you to know," he said, "how lucky you are." (My mother wept in the corner with her apron over her head.) Selfish young man as I was then, I tended to think that I had made my own luck, although my father's story moved me, of course it did, but what, really, did it have to do with me?

George: He was a good man, Thomas Freeman; I did everything I could to help him. And then, he caused me all that trouble.

Letty

IN THE EVENINGS, AFTER DINNER, I read over what I'd written in the day, or perused a book, while George played his fiddle. I took an intense dislike to "The Lament of Flora Macdonald." He said he loved those old Jacobite tunes, so mournful, most of them, but they pierced his heart.

I had never cared for fiddle music; I'm not the least bit musical myself, as several music masters discovered early in my childhood. Couldn't paint watercolours, couldn't play an étude by Chopin or anyone else. I still remember an amusing conversation I had with my Yorkshire cousins the first time I visited them as a young woman.

"Do you paint?" they asked.

"No."

"Do you play the harp or the piano?"

"I'm afraid not."

"Embroider?"

"No, again."

"Crewel work?"

I shook my head.

"I write," I said.

Although they weren't very interested in what I wrote ("We never read novels"), I think Julia, the eldest, was quite relieved. Perhaps she thought she would have to teach me my ABCs.

By the time of my death I had grown to loathe George's fiddle and rather hoped the white ants would be attracted and make a meal of it. And although I was a regular night owl back home, by ten o'clock I was ready for sleep. I'm not sure when George slept, if ever, for when I went to my own rooms I could often hear the faint strains of "The Braes of Killiecrankie" come floating through the air. I also know that even when he quit the fiddle-playing, he often ascended to a tower room he called "the cockloft" where he kept his telescope and maps.

No wonder he found it difficult to get up in the morning. If he hadn't had such a strong sense of duty, I doubt if he would have risen before noon. (By noon, if I attempted to write a letter, I perspired so much I had to put little arrows to the margins with "Not tears! Not tears!" to explain away the smudges.)

The Dutch governor of Elmina Castle volunteered a visit. He came, with his aide-de-camp, in complete regalia. You can imagine my anxieties. A dinner party for the local merchants and others was easy compared to this. However, I believe it went off smoothly; the old man was very gallant, even if his English left something to be desired. It sounded very much like Oom Kroop de Poop. George had made his special rum punch, which was indulged in before dinner. I think the men out here will use any excuse to make a toast. The Queen, of course, but sunrise, sunset, moonrise, moonset, perhaps the birds in the trees, the snakes on the ground. Always "absent friends."

The next morning George could not get up at all. I'd ascribe some of it to the "flowing bowl" and all the wine at dinner, but much of it to that uniform in that heat. His tunic was a very tropic in itself. I was mortally embarrassed to have to preside over the breakfast table by myself, but the old gentleman very kindly pretended nothing was amiss.

I never did get to see Elmina Castle, although it is only seven miles away. The Portuguese built it and Brodie said its name means, "the mine" because of all the gold they hoped to find there. He also said there was a ladder in the old slaving days and a trap door that led from the courtyard to the governor's quarters. The female slaves would be assembled and the governor, from his balcony, looked down and chose the one he desired. If the woman became pregnant, she was set free. There are many children and grandchildren of these women in Elmina town. Did the same thing go on at Anamaboe or Cape Coast Castle? I asked. No, he said, only at Elmina. (Did the terrified women stand there, hoping to be chosen?)

I had a child once. I gave it away. I have to say "it" in order to think of that time at all.

Those awful scandal sheets, particularly *The Wasp*, were horribly close to the mark when they said I went away into the country stout and returned my usual slim self. (Although I was never sylph-like. "Pleasingly plump" the Misses Lance used to say.)

It was arranged that I should go to a convalescent home in the Cotswolds, a village with the ominous name of Lower Slaughter. There, after I was registered under an assumed name, he kissed me on my cheek, said, "Be a brave little soldier," and left me. We had agreed there would be no communication between us during the weeks I was away until the manager of the home contacted him through a third party.

Outside of a stroll around the grounds twice a day, there was really nothing to do. This was not a place where one struck up instant friendships. How I longed for London and conversation. I felt the way I had in Paris when Miss Turin, my companion, was bedridden and dear Mr. Heine came to call. He inquired, in beautiful French, if I had been to the shops, the Jardin des Plantes, the opera, the theatres, had I made the promenade? After each question I sadly replied, *"Mais non."*

Finally, in desperation he said, *"Mais mademoiselle, qu'est qu'elle a fait?"*

"Mais ... mais ... j'ai regardé par la fenêtre."

I had a few books with me, of course, but I couldn't settle to anything. All I could do was lie on the sofa and curse my fate. The house was extremely quiet, quiet as the tomb, you might say, although there were the occasional dreadful distant screams and the sound of hurrying feet. I needed someone to talk to. I was a prisoner there for over two months and I hated everything about it: Matron's cheerful, "And how are we this morning?"; the banal chatter of the aides who walked me around the gardens and asked if I enjoyed knitting; the bland food. Most of all I hated the man who was responsible for my being in this place.

Needless to say, I couldn't write; what would I write about? "Ode to the Counterpane"? "Sonnet On the Breakfast Tray"? I did try, wrote the beginnings of a piece on solitude, but my brain wasn't up to it.

One morning the staff nurse came in to tell me, "We've had twins this morning, lovely boys."

I asked her politely not to disturb me with news reports of what went on elsewhere in the nursing home.

"I'm sorry, I'm sure," she said, and flounced out.

Later, I think she took pleasure in the fact that my labour was so long and painful.

("What is that cry?"

"It is the cry of women, my good Lord.")

When my time came, I asked to have a silk scarf tied around my eyes, for I did not want to see it. I was in Hell for twenty-four hours and they feared for my life. I bit my lip clear through and begged for them to kill me. When it was over and I heard the baby's cry, I fell back senseless.

By the time they had revived me, it had been taken away.

William came the next day. "I've made all the arrangements," he said, "there's nothing for you to worry about now. Just stay here and rest until you are strong enough to return."

I said nothing and refused to look at him.

"Poor Letty," he said, but when he went to stroke my hair I slapped his hand away.

"Don't touch me."

At the door he turned. "I gave her a name."

I clapped my hands over my ears. "Go away!"

"Laura," he said, "as you're so fond of Petrarch."

I began to scream and a nurse rushed in.

"What have you done to upset her?"

"Nothing," he said, "she is prone to hysterics, poor girl. I'll leave her now."

As soon as I could manage to walk from the bed to the window, I rang for the matron and said my "father" (the mistake was initially hers, but we had decided it was a useful pretense) had brought me a letter the day he visited and I was instructed to go directly to my uncle's home in Yorkshire as soon as I was well enough to travel.

"You are too weak, still, to travel such a distance by yourself; surely your father or mother should accompany you."

"My mother is dead; my father has had to leave for the Continent."

"I think, then, you should wait another fortnight at the very least."

"I can't wait any longer. Please arrange a seat in the coach and ask the maid to pack my trunk."

"This is against my wishes; you do understand that?"

I absolved her and her precious "Home" of any responsibility and the next day I was carried down the stairs and placed in their private, closed carriage which would connect me with the coach.

The journey north was a nightmare and I was nearly weeping by the time I reached my uncle's house. How startled he looked to see this half-dead woman pounding on his door at dusk. He did not even recognize me at first.

"Yes?" And then, "For Heaven's sake, Letty!"

At which point I fell senseless at his feet.

I told my aunt, a kindly and circumspect woman, that I had undergone an operation for a "female complaint" and had fled the hospital because I couldn't stand the noise and smells. She did not believe me, but she never questioned me, just put me to bed with hot water bottles to stop my shivering.

My uncle wanted to call a doctor immediately, but somehow she persuaded him not to, said that all I needed was rest and nourishment. Men, unless they *are* doctors, are reluctant to inquire too closely into women's illnesses and so the doctor was never called.

I sent a note to William at his office.

> Dear Sir:
>
> I caught a chill and so am spending a somewhat longer time than originally planned at my uncle's in Yorkshire. I will contact you when I return to London. I do realize I must continue to rely on you for commissions to write reviews, etc. and for some help with the business side of things, but other than that I feel our friendship is at an end. I am afraid I have relied on you too heavily in the past and it has caused talk; this talk has caused me pain. A woman alone has to be very careful of her reputation; I'm sure you understand this, being an "honourable man," yourself.
>
> L.E.L.

After that I simply let myself recover. Such an interesting word — something one does to shabby settees and chairs: re-cover. Also to worn-out bodies and souls. (I am not sure either completely recovered from that terrible experience.)

Thanks to basins of gruel and buckets of broth, I was finally able to take meals with the family. My uncle had four daughters, two of whom were now married and living in Scarborough, "the Paradise of the North"; the other two were just waiting their turn.

We had prayers every morning and night — all knelt except the invalid — and readings from the Bible. I felt I laid up such a stock of good behaviour during that fortnight in Yorkshire, that I might be forgiven for at least some of my sins.

The Misses Lance, their ancient papa and the other boarders were delighted to have me back.

"Oh, Letty, how we missed you!"
I had one rather mean letter from W.J. waiting for me on my return.

> I made you, you know. You were just a plump lit-
> tle girl rolling a hoop when you lived next door, a
> plump little girl whose cousin sent me some vers-
> es by you, desiring my opinion. There was a spark,
> certainly, of something, in those juvenile efforts,
> but it was I who fanned that spark into a flame, who
> edited and corrected and encouraged. Don't you
> ever forget that. You and I share many bonds that
> can't be broken.
>> Kindest regards,
>> Wm. Jerdan

Henceforth I only communicated with him by letter. What arro-
gance! "Made" me, indeed. What a puffed-up little man. Any traces
of affection I still felt for him vanished forever.

Mr. Freeman

I DID ENJOY BEING A GARDENER and had imagined I would probably re-main at Orwell Park until rheumatism forced me to retire. I even had a sweetheart. Then one Sunday afternoon, in a motley crowd, my life took a different direction; I stopped to hear a man preaching under a tree. For the first time I understood that God belonged to everyone, or rather, that God cared for everyone, and cared about us equally. I had never felt that before, growing up as I did with one foot in Africa and the other foot in England. I was always a misfit, even more than my father, who at least was purely black. I was "the mulatto." I knew my suffering was as the bite of a gnat compared to the suffering of my father and the thousands like him, but to a small child, and then a growing lad, looking different is very hard. My village would have shown me more kindness if I had been the local idiot.

And then, this revelation: all souls who accepted Christ Jesus were shining white! Money meant nothing in the grand scheme of things; position meant nothing. I scarcely remember now what the man said, but he was so full of conviction and contentment that I went back to my quarters a different man.

I began attending these al fresco gatherings whenever I could and in due course this got back to Sir Robert. One morning he stopped me as I was suckering the tomato plants.

"Are you become one of those Wesleyan, Thomas?"

"I think so, Sir Robert. I do believe I'm headed in that direction."

"Well, if that is really the case then you will soon be heading away from Orwell Park. We can't have Dissenters here. At some point you will have to choose. I'll tell you frankly that you are the best head gardener we have ever employed and it would be hard, if not impossible, to replace you. But I mean what I say. If you keep on in this way you can't stay here."

I knew there was really no choice — my heart had already declared for the Methodists. Within a month I was headed for London with my small satchel of books and my even smaller hoard of savings. I presented myself at the offices of the Wesleyan Society and begged them to train me as a lay preacher. Thanks to my mother, I knew my Bible well, and my parents had presented me with a Bible of my own when I first left home. The Wesleyans were impressed by my enthusiasm, I could see that right away, and after catechizing me with hard questions, they were even more impressed.

"Thomas," said one of my inquisitors (how lovely it was to hear my name spoken with such warmth!), "Thomas, I think you are just the man for us. But I also think you may have a higher calling than simply roaming the countryside and preaching under a tree. I think you might consider training to be a missionary."

I knew what he was going to say, but still I had to ask.

"A missionary, Sir? In what part of the world?"

"Africa."

(Of course.)

At first I was rather downcast, but tried not to show it. Were they sending me to Africa because they suspected no one would listen to me here in England? Were they sending me "back where I belonged"? I decided to put the matter in God's hands and God let me know He didn't think much of my whinging. There was one thing, however, I felt I should insist upon. I told the committee I had a sweetheart back at Orwell Park, a strong young woman to whom I was almost engaged to be married. I had told her that if I got on in my new avocation I would send for her. If, after my training, I was to be sent out to Africa, I should like to marry her and take her with me.

"Is she devout?"

"She is, but not yet a Wesleyan."

"Would she be willing to take instruction?"

"I believe so."

"Then, providing she pledges herself to Methodism and to missionary work, we can think of no objection."

I wrote to her that night in care of her sister, who lived in a neighbouring village. I wrote with excitement and love; I could see our lives unfolding like the lives of my parents — a diorama of marital happiness and mutual comfort.

I did not know I was taking her to her death.

George

WHEN LETTY TOLD ME HOW IRRITATED she would get by the sound of Mrs. Bailey's knitting needles, I thought that her chatter was sometimes like that, for me, and once or twice (she was a great chatterer in bed) I had such a temptation to put my hand over her mouth. Not to hurt her, you understand, merely to shut her up. Chatter chatter chatter. It's strange, is it not, how the things that initially attract you to someone — in Letty's case her openness, her lively mind — can, later on, nearly drive you mad. No doubt things that I did drove her mad as well.

Letty: I hated our damp bodies touching one another. After I shared the conjugal bed in Africa for a while, I was amazed to think of all those families with hordes of children. I suppose the heat doesn't affect them in the same way and Brodie said large families are very important out here — the sign of a man's potency. And I doubt if a native woman has the option of a separate sleeping room or a door she can close. I know George thought that I was unresponsive, too "refined" to enjoy the carnal act, but that wasn't it at all. It was too hot, too *slippery*, unpleasant in that sense. I suppose his African wench hadn't minded skin sticking to skin, sheets so damp afterwards you could almost wring them out. Mrs. Bailey told me that natives do it the way dogs do it. I told her I didn't want to listen to such coarse talk, but I expect it's true.

I asked Brodie if love meant anything to them, whether it was a sentiment they understood.

He smiled: "If you mean *our* ideas of love — romance and so on — probably not. But they can feel passionately about another person and jealousy is not unknown to them. The ju-ju stalls in the markets are full of potions and powders and dried things to punish the rival or sometimes to do away with him or her (mostly her, I think) altogether. And surely you've seen the affection they have for their children?

They are not afraid to show it, unlike our northern races. And haven't you noticed, when you walk through the town, that you rarely hear a child crying? Perhaps if he has sustained a small injury he will cry for a minute or two, but then he is up and running again."

"I don't get a chance to walk through the town very often; George doesn't like me to wander about. I do know the children here are very bold. I don't think much of their manners. They follow me."

"Oh, they follow you because you fascinate them. They are not used to seeing white women, except for the few missionary wives, but they die off so quickly. It's just curiousity."

"They call me a ghost. They point at me and laugh at me. I so dislike being laughed at."

"It's all good-natured, really it is."

"Sometimes I have this terrible urge to slap one or two of them."

"I'm surprised to hear that."

"Why surprised? It seems quite a normal reaction to ridicule."

"They are children."

"I dislike children at the best of times, but when a little crocodile of piccaninnies follows me, pointing and jeering, my dislike intensifies."

"Perhaps you would think differently if . . . ." He blushed, so I knew what he was thinking.

"I doubt it. At any rate, my books are my progeny."

"Of course."

As soon as we had drunk our tea, he left. I knew I would get a note, delivered by one of Mr. Topp's boys, saying how he had overstepped the bounds of friendship and would I forgive him? Of course I would forgive him. What would I do without him? Yet his words had hurt. Not a mortal wound, more like a paper cut. They stung.

I tried never to think of that time but she was there, somewhere deep down, squalling, as I lay there with a silk bandage wound tightly against my eyes: Laura.

George: Brodie Cruickshank. I think he was more than a little in love with her.

Letty: Tell me, Mr. Freeman, what do you imagine Heaven to be like?
   Freeman: If Hell is all searing hotness, I would expect a more temperate clime. (Laughing. Hee hee. Showing his strong white teeth.)

Letty

"AND WHEN YOU ARE FINISHED, George, what then?"

He was eating half a paw-paw, scraping out the shiny black seeds, which always reminded me of ants. He squeezed half a lime over the orange meat, ready to dig in.

"What then?"

"Yes. When you retire. Will you go back to Scotland, spend your days fishing or reading, perhaps writing an account of your years on the Gold Coast?"

I could see myself in a cozy parlour, writing, while George was doing the same in his study. A cozy parlour not too far from Edinburgh, I hoped. I would need Society. (And with the success of my book on Scott and perhaps my romance about the freed slave woman from Elmina, I would have a secure place there as Letitia Landon, as well as Mrs. George Maclean.)

"I will die here, Letty, I have no intention of settling in Scotland or anywhere else. This is where I belong; this is where I will be buried." He squeezed the lime so hard it squirted him in the face.

That night, when he reached for me, I turned my back. I had never seen marriage to George as permanent exile. There were scores of Army, Navy, what have you in pleasant retirement in London or the Home Counties. Who on earth would ever want to stay out here forever? I could accept Edinburgh instead of London as my final destination, but Cape Coast? Fine for a few years — I was writing well, had become quite efficient at being the chatelaine of the castle, but I needed conversation, admiration, social interaction. It had never occurred to me that George didn't need those things or felt his role as governor was enough. I was already worried about what would become of me when Brodie went on leave. I knew George and I had our "If she doesn't like it, she can leave after three years" agreement, but I *did* like it, most of the time; I just couldn't see me burying myself out here forever.

A few days later I talked to Brodie. "Are you planning to stay out here forever?"

"I doubt it; why do you ask?"

"The other night George said he will stay here until he dies."

"Oh, but George is a special case."

"How so?"

"I'm not sure I can explain it. There are certain men who 'find themselves' in places like this. I think George is one."

"You mean he has some ideal self he is trying to live up to?"

"Something like that, but not exactly."

"What then?"

"I really don't know how to put it."

"And you — you don't have this?"

"No. Not at all."

"You must have had it once, or you wouldn't be here."

"Possibly. Not anymore."

We left it at that.

George

LETTY WANTED A PICNIC. I couldn't really spare the time, but she so rarely asked anything of me I felt I should indulge her. "If you can arrange the 'wittles,'" I said, "then I can arrange the rest. I suggest we set out after the heat of the day."

Beyond the town, the bush extends on three sides. On the fourth is the Castle and the sea. But at the rear of the town a path had been cut long ago; it led past the graveyard and so it was not a route one would take by choice. The graves of the little band of Wesleyans who had disembarked with Mr. Freeman the previous January were already completely covered over with vines and vegetation. It is rather terrifying the way things seem to spring up here overnight. No, past the graveyard would not have been the first choice, except that it was the only choice for an excursion with a picnic — the only way we could take the road west to the salt pond about three-quarters of a mile away.

I suggested Mrs. Bailey and Letty be carried there in litters.

Letty: We set off around three, although it was still very warm. If we had left it any later we'd not get back before dark. Mr. Freeman was of the party and Brodie, Mr. Swanzy, Mr. Hutton, Mr. William Topp, and his heavily pregnant native wife. I felt quite strange to be riding whilst she was walking and Mrs. Bailey offered to give up her place, but Mrs. Topp smiled and said no, that it was "no trouble a-tall" and she preferred to walk.

My bearers were the same giants who had carried me ashore when I arrived. They were so tall that I looked down on the walkers' heads and could see the sovereign-sized bald spot which was forming on the top of George's head. (He was not wearing his topi as we weren't in direct sunlight.)

The litter was a sort of basket-work affair made of wicker-work with a palm-leaf mattress, a cross between a trug and a butcher's basket —

not very pleasant really, as one was jolted from side to side. The men all carried thin bamboo canes with which they beat at the bushes on either side. The path was quite broad, but it was bordered with dense brush where venomous snakes could be resting. George had assured me that for the most part the snakes stayed out of the way. (Men going abroad at night stamp their feet to let the snakes know they are passing.)

Swish. Swish. Swish. And then a sharp cry from Mr. Freeman who was out in front. "Halt!"

A wriggling green mass lay in the middle of the road ahead. Baby mambas, Mr. Topp informed me: "They don't know enough to get out of the way." *Swish swish swish* went Mr. Freeman's cane and the babies were quickly dispatched.

"Were they poisonous?" I inquired of Mr. Topp.

"Not yet, no. But very poisonous when grown. Fatal."

Mr. Freeman pushed the broken green bits off to the side and we proceeded.

After that there were no more incidents and soon we arrived at a clearing above the salt pond — which was much bigger than I had imagined it — and Isaac and two other sense boys who had gone on ahead, spread cushions and rugs and then produced from their hampers a veritable feast of cold fowl, tomatoes, cucumbers, fresh bread, and punch.

Déjeuner sur l'herbe. I noticed that most of the party ate with their hands so I proceeded to do the same, hoping this would not be my first step on the road to "going native." A clay pot of water and clean towels cleansed our fingers when we had finished the main course. We followed with those small sweet bananas they call "white man's fingers" and pieces of fresh coconut.

"Beauty is deceptive, is it not?" said Mr. Freeman, lounging on one elbow. "That vine in the distance, for instance, whose lovely white flowers will begin to unfold when darkness fall: *datura stramonium.*

Every bit of it is poison. When the flowers are open, they emit a pleasing fragrance and they are fed upon by moths. It is sometimes called devil's trumpet. No doubt it is on offer at the ju-ju stall, as pills or potion. Perhaps you have seen it in England?

"Is it similar to the morning glory? "

"Similar and yet not. The seeds contain a deadly poison and the juice of the seeds, I have heard, is one way to get rid of an enemy. Isn't that true, Mrs. Topp?"

"Very true," she said, "but there are many such things. We call them 'medicine.' Some harm; some heal.

"The trial of the snake's teeth

"The boiling palm-oil test

"The poison nut

"The calabar bean."

"Of course," said Mr. Freeman, twirling his plucked flower between thumb and finger, "we have deadly plants in England as well. The leaves of the lowly rhubarb, for instance, will kill a child, the seeds of the laburnum tree, the pretty digitalis. I think I could make up a nice sermon on the deceptiveness of beauty — how one shouldn't trust it, what do you think?"

"I think," said I, "that you enjoyed whacking those baby mambas. Was that a Biblical fury, Mr. Freeman, because of the damage done by the serpent in the Garden? Could you not make a sermon out of that? The canes of Righteousness, perhaps? Or perhaps, because Mr. Topp has informed me that the baby mambas are not poisonous, the Sins of the Fathers?"

"You are teasing me, Mrs. Maclean."

"And you have been trying to frighten me, I think."

George told me later that he thought I had gone too far, but I didn't care. The missionary bothered me with his big smile and his ingratiating ways. And I disliked the way he spoke to Isaac and the other boys. Or snapped his fingers at them. Or clapped his hands. "Boy! You, Boy!"

And I know he thought me silly, frivolous even. He might have approved of Milton, or Dante with his concept of the beautiful lie, but for a woman to write poetry just for the sake of writing poetry, novels ditto — novels! — with no aim of leading the mind up to God, well, how frivolous can you get? I once told him I took my writing very seriously.

"I know you do," he said. And sighed.

Mr. Freeman

"DEAD TO GOD AND ASLEEP IN THE ARMS OF SATAN": that is how Charles Wesley described himself as a youth. How much more does this apply to the Fantee people? And it is not as though one had a clean slate to write upon. No No No No No. So many rituals, so much mumbo-jumbo; so many fetishes and taboos. But, with God's help, we shall overcome.

Letty

THERE IS NO TWILIGHT ON THE COAST, no "fairy web of night and day."
Night comes swiftly, like a dark curtain drawn across the sky. I missed
the twilight; in London I had always loved the hours between five and
seven; it was a magical time. I called them, "the hours of possibility."
Who knew what might happen later on? Of course there was work
to be done: clothes must be considered, jewellery scrutinized, hair
dressed. There was the mask that one always wears when venturing
forth into Society; that must be firmly fixed in place. There was always
someone who took my success as a personal affront, some second-
rate poet who still dined out on a slim volume published years ago,
for instance. "Mmmmm — Miss Landon. Of course I never read you,
but my old aunt thinks you are wonderful." That sort of thing. You
must never show that you are at all vulnerable, and fortunately I was
quick: "Oh *do* introduce me to your aunt! She must be so proud of
your little book. Are you working on another?"

And we dined at such an outrageous time in the Castle. I had a
small sherry and George a large whiskey at seven and then we went
in to dinner. If we were hosting a dinner party, then of course we
dined much later, but most days our preprandial, prandial, and post
prandial activities were over fairly quickly and without a great deal
of that spice to the sauce — a lively conversation. I asked him about
his day, which was mostly spent adjudicating between claims and
counter-claims of a most ridiculous sort: two men both claimed ownership of a shirt; "a certain man" had put "medicine" in the plaintiff's
soup, medicine meaning poison. He asked me about my day. Perhaps
we strolled along the battlements, had a quick look at the moon if the
clouds had moved away, then George excused himself and went up to
his "cockloft" where he played with his telescope, wrote up reports,
or practised some air on his fiddle.

I read — I was re-reading all of the Waverly novels — and later
joined him in our apartments. I rarely stayed through the night.

It was not that George was stupid, but in many ways he lacked imagination (or the painter's eye, which is very like the poet's).

> A primrose by the river's brim
> A yellow primrose was to him
> But it was nothing more.

He does have a romantic ideal of himself he must live up to, he must be seen always as a fair man, and just. People walk miles to have him hear of their complaints; there is always a crowd before the gates are opened in the morning.

In my letters home I sometimes "doctored" his dinnertime reports — suggested that he thought for a minute of playing Solomon and offering to rip the shirt in two and thus find out the true owner. I suppose I wanted to build him up in the eyes of my friends. We all do that, don't we, build people up or tear them down, whichever suits our purpose. (Not George, though, never George. He did no building-up or tearing-down. One of the things I so admired about him was his honesty.)

Letty

It is taboo for the fishermen to fish on Tuesdays, the agriculturalists to dig or plant on Fridays. And so they work on Sundays, which is the Christian day of rest. Mr. Freeman says all that must change or, at the very least, they must not work on Sundays once they convert. This was met with great resentment. Why should they lose two days of work? Then give up the old taboos, says Mr. Freeman, but they are frightened to do so. There is an eye painted on the prow of the canoes, and the words ONYAME NAA, "God never sleeps." But which God?

To make matters worse, there was a drowning in mid-September. The fishermen cannot swim, so if a canoe capsizes and they can't hang on until another canoe comes to their rescue, they drown. Do they cry out? If, as Brodie told me, the women are not allowed to cry out when giving birth, are the men supposed to be equally brave — or do they pray and scream in those panic-stricken moments before they let go and are swallowed by the hungry sea? I once met a general who had been in the Peninsula War. He said most dying men call for their mothers, particularly the young lads. In this case all the men were saved except one.

They brought his body up from the beach and paraded it through the town. That night the drums went on until dawn and there was much weeping and wailing. Mr. Freeman stayed inside the mission house; the boy was one of his converts.

I meant to ask Mrs. Bailey if sailors can swim. If not, how naive to trust that your ship will never let you down. My own experience at sea almost convinced me that I could never go on board a ship again; I would have to stay here forever. Which is what happened, isn't it? My letters went home, my essays, even my trunks, but not me.

The fish here is wonderful. A fish dinner, with roasted yams and plantain fried in palm oil is Heaven. But George is a hearty eater; he wants some sort of stew or roasted meat to follow and a pudding to follow that. He will be corpulent later on, but perhaps not. Except for the governor of Elmina, the white men I have seen so far are all thin, weedy, most of them.

Brodie said the men need exercise; he worked with Indian clubs every morning when he was at Anamaboe and in Accra, he said, there are tennis courts. Perhaps we could have a clay court here, I said, but would George play tennis? Somehow I doubted it.

Sometimes, when George and I met up for a "wee dram" before dinner (whiskey for him, ginger beer or sherry for me) he would look at me in puzzlement and blink his eyes once or twice. I think for a moment he had no idea who I was. Then his face would clear; ah, yes, the wife.

I made sure that the table was set properly every evening: silver, crystal, candles, hibiscus flowers floating in a glass bowl, my Grandmother Bishop's damask tablecloth. He never commented on any of this; I doubt he even noticed it, and yet I'm sure this was all new to him out here. The one thing he always praised was the pudding. Thanks to Mrs. Bailey, Ibrahim now had quite a repertoire of stodge.

One afternoon I took a walk down to the beach with Mrs. Bailey and Isaac. She had a mind to see if she could buy directly from the fishermen rather than wait for tomorrow's market. The fishermen chant as they haul the nets up onto the shore. The market women are congregated there with their baskets and after they have bargained, they raise the loaded baskets to their heads and walk away like queens. Everything is carried on the head, enormous loads, yet they have beautiful posture. It was very colourful — the women in their cloths of many colours, the men chanting, the wind blowing, the tall palm trees like one-legged birds or feather dusters. I wrote to Maclise (he painted me, you know — a very flattering portrait) and said he should arrange a visit, for there was much here to interest the painter's eye. A little ragged boy separated himself from his companions ("Bronie, Bronie, Bronie, give me dashee-o") came up to me and put his hand in mine. Just for a moment he let it rest there and smiled up at me. I think the others dared him to do it. Then he ran, laughing, back to his "gang." Something stirred in me, some swift yearning, almost a pain in my heart.

I wonder if George ever wanted children. When I first came I noticed several children with rusty hair and rather blotchy skin. I wondered if those were George's by-blows, but Mrs. Bailey (who had obviously wondered the same thing) said Isaac had told her that these children have some disease that makes them like that. There is no cure, but the surgeon intends to take one or two of them to London when he next goes on leave. He wants to show them to some colleague of his who specializes in tropical medicine. After all, he said, who would have dreamt that something as simple as limes would be the answer to scurvy? I liked Mr. Cobbold; he was so good when George was ill. But by not performing an autopsy on me he certainly put the cat among the pigeons.

Mr. Freeman

I SAW MRS. MACLEAN OUT WALKING with Mrs. Bailey and their young servant. Our lady of leisure. I wished she would show some interest in the day-to-day struggles of our mission. She said she had "commitments" to publishers in London and must finish certain things before the ship arrives. I had dipped into her work — such a lot of words to cover so very little substance. Not my dish of tea. *Never mind,* I said to myself, *God will give me the help I need* — *"the back is made for the burden."*

I did miss my wife. She nursed me through my fever and then she sickened. The night before she died, not having spoken or opened her eyes for hours, she suddenly sat bolt upright in bed, cried out "My God! My God!" then seized my hand, and looking directly at me, she said, "Thomas, this time tomorrow I shall be in Heaven."

I will need another wife and have written to the Society for someone suitable. Meanwhile, the merchants are convivial, the new chapel comes on apace and Captain Maclean supports me in every way. The fowls we were given when we arrived were thriving and I started a little vegetable garden out by the cemetery, for I would like to be self-sufficient.

I must tell you an amusing story, which I related to my friends over a glass or two of punch. One afternoon, as I was returning to the house after my labours, a young girl greeted me and said she had been sent to me.

"Do you wish to learn about the Christian God?" I asked. The more young women I could convert, the easier my task would be. The women will persuade the men, for no mission girl would want to marry a pagan, and no young man would want to see his sweetheart pledge her troth to another.

"No, Sah. I be sent for you. I be wife — for *you.*"

Well, you can imagine my shock! I quickly sent her back home to her Mama.

The men laughed and laughed (I must admit I exaggerated my fa-
cial expressions as I told this tale), but then Mr. Swanzy said,

"You do realize, old chum, that you have shamed her?"

"How so? I would have shamed her by taking her in."

"That's according to your view; but according to theirs, you sent
her back because she was not good enough. I should imagine she was
beaten when she returned."

"Surely not."

"Surely so."

I was terribly distressed to hear this and prevailed upon Swanzy,
who was an Old Coaster and spoke the language like a native, to find
out where the girl lived and explain to her parents that my God did
not allow me to take a concubine.

"Don't you get lonely, Thomas?"

"Of course; I'm a man, aren't I? But I will soon have a second wife
who will be joined to me in Christian marriage."

"Good luck to you, then."

Letty

THE RAINS VIRTUALLY STOPPED by the first week in October and the red dust blew into and onto everything, every nook and cranny, every fold and pleat. It blotted my writing, it even got between my teeth. If anything was set out early, on the dinner table, it had to be covered over with fine net cloches. I was surprised, on the occasions when George and I lay together, that we didn't act as emery boards to one another. When I first arrived I thought the contrast of the red earth and the lush green hills was picturesque in the extreme; now I hated it. I could sponge myself off two or three times a day and yet I never felt refreshed. I became nostalgic for the rains, but everyone else said the Dry Season was the healthy season, or as healthy as it gets — out here.

The wind blew all the time, day and night. The wind in the palm trees rattled the leaves like bones. The wind blew and the waves crashed against the shore, the drums went on, distant or up close (someone was "wedded or deaded" as Mrs. Bailey used to say), and I found it hard to sleep. Some nights I could hear an animal screaming; it sounded like a child being murdered, awful. I told George and he said it was a little creature called a hyrax, a kind of sloth, and the natives had a folk tale about it which involved Anansi the Spider-Man.

"I can't remember exactly what the hyrax did to provoke Anansi, but he did *something*, and Anansi the Spider set out after him.

"'Say you're sorry or *you'll* be sorry,' Anansi yelled.

"Seeing a palm tree close by, the hyrax scrambled a little ways up.

"'I'm sorry,' he said.

"'Again,' said Anansi.

"'I'm sorry.' (And the hyrax climbed a little higher up the tree.)

"And so it went on, with Anansi standing at the bottom of the tall coconut palm and the hyrax calling out, 'Sorry Sorry Sorry' until he made his way to the very top. *Then* he changed his tune, knowing that the spider could never reach him.

"'I'm not sorry!' he screamed. 'I'm not sorry! I'm not sorry!' And that is what you've been hearing.

"The people love stories about Anansi, grown-ups as well as children. He's naughty, and he's a shape-shifter. He can turn himself into anything: a piece of cloth, a log, a sleeping-mat."

"A sleeping-mat?"

"Oh, yes. He likes playing tricks on people and on animals. I'll see if I can remember more of them. Someone should collect them and write them down in English. Now there's a job for you, Letty. The thing is, they are not really Fantee stories, they come from the Ashantee people, but they have made their way down to the Coast."

"With the slaves, I suppose."

"I suppose so."

"Well how do I get the hyrax to stop screaming?"

"You don't. Just wait for him to move on."

Letty

FOR THE FIRST SEVERAL DAYS, except for nursing George AND the awkward visit from the Governor of Elmina Castle, I lived in almost complete seclusion, but I had great resources in my writing (which I did for a few hours every day while my husband slept) and I remained quite well. I did miss flattery (I've never pretended I wasn't vain) but even more I missed talking about ideas and books. Then Brodie arrived.

At the end of our second week a delightful young man came to see me, or rather, he initially came to pay his respects to George and to welcome me — he said he was quite a fan of my work. Brodie Cruickshank, head of Anamaboe Fort some miles beyond Elmina. Another Scot and a fellow student of my husband's when he was at Elgin Academy. But very different from George, oh yes.

George was still unwell and unable to receive him, so I did the honours. I thought it was very rude of George not to make the effort, when Mr. Cruickshank had come all that way to see him, and he, too, had been ill, he said, and was still suffering from headache.

We lunched together and chatted about all sorts of things. He had read nearly all of my books and confessed, shyly, that he had come to meet the wonderful L.E.L. just as much as he had come to welcome the governor home. Just before he left he took a small volume from his breast pocket.

"Would you autograph this for me?" He was to stay a few days at Mr. Topp's and asked permission to call on me again.

I hoped he would stay a fortnight — forever! After he left I realized that I had lived the past few weeks in virtual silence. George was simply not a talker. Getting a conversation going with him was a task equal to that of the Israelites making bricks out of straw. That was just how he was, and to add to that, he was still feeling rotten. I needed the attention I received that afternoon from Brodie Cruickshank; I was parched for it. Mrs. Bailey likes to say she'd "murder for a cup of tea." Well I was ready to murder for a real conversation! For recognition that I was important in my own right; flattery; laughter: I gulped it down, felt quite dizzy with it all, as though it had been wine, not words. Brodie — he had asked me to call him Brodie — seemed more English than Scotch, perhaps a little French as well. People back home said I, too, had a French "flavour."

George: Brodie Cruickshank. A nice enough fellow, good at his job. I think he was a little bit in love with Letty.

Mr. Freeman: Mr. Topp had a visitor, the Head of Anamaboe fort, farther along the coast. He had just called at the Castle and reported that Governor Maclean was still convalescing and unable to see him until tomorrow. However, he had lunched with Mrs. Maclean and all of his talk was of her. Did we realize that she was the premier poetess of England? Didn't we think it amazing that she was here on the coast? How brave of her to come etc. etc. etc.

Mr. Cruickshank was quite yellow about the eyeballs and he did say he'd had fever recently and was still suffering from headaches. However, he would be going on leave in October and a few months of Highland air would soon put him right.

He seemed a bit of a milksop — all this talk of poetry and headaches with a few French phrases thrown in. I wondered what he would think if I volunteered the fact that I could give the Latin names of just about anything growing here on the coast?

"Have you read L.E.L.'s poetry, Mr. Freeman?"

"I have glanced at it."

"Oh, you must do much more than glance at it; she has depths; she can move you to tears."

"I shall have to try again."

Mr. Topp's wife was an excellent cook. I took pains to complement her on the stew. Her marriage to William Topp was a Christian marriage and she was a strong supporter of my work. A beautiful woman, even when heavily with child as she was that night. I walked home under the stars, hoping I would soon hear from the Society about the possibility of another wife.

Letty: George said to me one evening in early October, "Why Letty, you look wonderful; you are positively blooming."

"Thank you, George," I said, "I do believe this climate agrees with me. And yet a little bird told me your friends were placing bets on how long I'd last."

George: Yes, I heard that rumour as well, but I don't believe it.

Letty: I shall have to observe who has the longest face and then I shall know which one wagered a guinea on "dead within a fortnight."

George: It was quite amazing. I had been unwell since the day we arrived — fever, chills, costiveness — and here was this London belle, this glasshouse flower, flourishing.

Mr. Freeman: All this young flesh, all this display, this ripeness. Testing me. God was testing me. But I could not help envying Mr. and Mrs. Topp and their obvious contentment.

Letty: I asked Mr. Freeman one day why he thought all the other missionaries died of fever when I had not even suffered from a touch of it.

"Perhaps because you live at the Castle, on higher ground."

"Then George should have been spared illness as well. And you, you live in town."

"I believe I was spared because God has plans for me."

"I see."

Freeman: She smiled and a little dimple appeared at the side of her cheek.

"And does God have plans for me, then?"

"I am not privy to God's plans."

Letty: "Ah," said Mr. Freeman, dining with us one evening, "Gentlemen's Relish, how wonderful!" Rubbing his hands together. How badly he wanted to be one of us.

George: Letty went on and on about Brodie Cruickshank.

Letty: "It's hard to believe you grew up in the same area. Brodie is so outgoing and you are so … taciturn."

George: "I told her I couldn't change who I was, 'not even for you.'"

"Oh, no, no. Please don't take offence. I like you just the way you are. But you know how one tends to generalize: the Irish, lovers of horses and stout, talkers, fiery; the French, fond of talk, witty, arrogant; the Scots — well, the Scots are more like you than Brodie Cruickshank."

"Perhaps he is the exception that proves the rule."

"Perhaps."

Letty: He stood up, throwing down his serviette. "Oh dear, I think I have hurt your feelings."

"Not at all. We true Scots have no feelings."

Letty: He went up to what he called his cockloft and that was the last I heard or saw of him that evening, although at one point, in the middle of the night, I thought there was someone outside my door.

"George?" "Isaac?" "Who's there?"

I shivered. Mrs. Bailey would have said, "Someone just walked over your grave."

Brodie Cruickshank

"MR. CRUICKSHANK," SHE SAID, "HOW DO YOU DO?" Her small hand in mine, such delicate bones. And her pale, pale skin, with the little blue vein just above the left temple. She was like some rare butterfly that had flown into the wrong garden; from the very first I feared for her health, yet she laughed when I told her this climate was deadly.

"Mr. Cruickshank, George told me the same thing, over and over and it's true, I've been a semi-invalid most of my life. At home I've often had to take to my bed, but here, for some reason, I thrive. I feel better than I have felt in years. It's you men who seem to suffer."

She was so good to me, bathing my forehead with eau de cologne, letting me lie on her settee while she sat next to me and read out bits from the essays she was writing on Walter Scott's female characters.

Letty: I had begun by writing from memory, but then dear Mr. Swanzy offered me a complete set that he had in his library. Who would have expected that from a hardened old merchant like himself? The bindings were falling apart and the pages were musty, but that didn't matter; the words were as fresh and beautiful as when I had encountered them for the first time

Brodie: "It is so good to hear the sound of an Englishwoman's voice."
Letty: Surely you would prefer a woman from your own country?

Brodie: I thought of Morag. Would I have wished Morag there, at that moment, in this charming sitting-room, on the coast of Western Africa? No — because if she were, then I would not be lying on Letty's settee. Morag was sensible and dear and I seriously thought about marrying her when I was home. But Letty ... when Letty brings a cool cloth to place on my aching head it is like a blessing.

Brodie: I don't think George cares for me very much; our interviews are very short.

Letty: Don't be silly; weren't you boyhood friends? He is so behind in his work he is abrupt with everyone, even me.

Brodie: I was closer to his brother Hugh, who is more outgoing. George was quite a solitary boy and he roomed with one of the masters; he rarely joined us day boys in our romps.

Letty: It is strange that you both ended up on the Coast.

Brodie: Not so strange, really. The world is peppered with transplanted Scotsmen. I think there is something restless built into our bones."

Brodie: The louvres were partially closed against the heat, but the sunlight still came in and lay thin bands of brightness across the room. I could hear the crashing of the sea down below.

Letty smiled and closed her writing folio. "That's enough of Jeanie Deans for today."

"I think these essays are turning out to be some of your best work so far."

"I think so, too. It's strange: I get so involved in the stories that I am truly transported to Scotland, or to Walter Scott's Scotland, for the truth is, I have never been north of my uncle's home in Yorkshire, that when I come out of this writing trance and look around me I'm not quite sure where I am. Perhaps someday I shall write about this Castle, and the sea, and that long line of coconut palms stretching all the way to Elmina — they look so much like tall, one-legged birds with all their feathers at the top. One night some sort of custom was going on, so I went outside and looked down at all those leaping and dancing and yelling figures, lit up by torchlight, and truly felt a thrill of the exotic, truly felt that I was in Africa. Most of the time, shut up here in the Castle, I don't feel that."

"Would you like to attend an Outdooring?"

"I might, if I knew what it was."

"When a child is born out here, it is kept inside for eight days and is not named during that time. This is because each living child has a ghost mother on the other side, who is calling for it to come back. After a week the ghost mother is presumed to have given up; the child is brought outside by the father and with a lot of ceremony the baby is given its name."

"Oh, I don't think so. You can come back and tell me all about it."

"That won't be the same as seeing it first-hand. Are you thinking you'll feel out of place?"

"It's partly that, yes."

"But I have been invited — I know the family quite well — and you will go as my guest. Would you like me to ask George if you can accompany me?"

"I'm quite free to come and go as I please." (Not quite the case, but this annoyed me, the idea that we would have to get George's permission.)

"Well then, bring your parasol and I will bring a canteen of fresh water and off we'll go. It's high time you saw some of the local customs."

Letty: I could think of no way to get out of this short of outright refusal, and so I went.

Letty

IT WAS A COLOURFUL SCENE; the paramount chief was there, in his splendid toga-like cloth made of bands of blue and orange interwoven with gold, sitting on a carved chair under a huge red silk umbrella with gold tassels hanging down, rather like a gigantic jellyfish. The chief wore a wreath of gold on his head and an awe-inspiring amount of gold bracelets, rings, and anklets adorned his person. Brodie said his feet are never allowed to touch the ground and so he is carried everywhere in a litter (I pitied the carriers; the old man must have weighed over twenty stone) and when he sits, his feet rest upon a little footstool. *The family must be people of consequence*, I thought, even though they appeared to live in one of those conical huts thatched with palm leaves that I had first thought were hayricks. Maybe this was just a ceremonial hut and they had a larger establishment elsewhere. The women wore sarongs of Manchester cloth in colours and patterns that dazzled the eye — red with green, yellow with blue, orange with blue; they seemed to have no colour sense whatsoever. The clothes of the men, woven in four-inch strips and in more subdued colours, were more to my taste. There was much talk and laughter and a real sense of anticipation as the gathering waited for the baby to appear. Brodie seemed to know a great many people and I was introduced to the most prominent of the old men, who smiled and nodded their woolly heads. He was just as fluent in the Fantee language as George.

Soon the door of the hut opened and we all grew silent, forming a kind of horseshoe on either side of the opening. Out came the father carrying the baby, naked except for a string of beads. One of the elders stepped forward, drank something from a calabash (I later learned it was rum) and spit directly into the child's mouth! I gasped, but no one else seemed to think this was disgusting. The baby was named by the father — Kudjoe something something — and then he was paraded around so we could all take a good look at him. A long table had been set up, with bottles of whiskey and clay pots of palm wine at one end, various delicacies in the middle, and a carved wooden bowl for presents of money at the other. Brodie gave a sovereign, I gave a bottle of whiskey on behalf of the Castle, and ten shillings on behalf of myself.

When the baby and his father had made the rounds, there was a call for silence and the chief's linguist stepped forward to announce the gift of two goats and five ounces of gold. (The chief never speaks to the people directly, but always through his linguist.) After that he was heaved into his litter and his retinue bore him away.

It is so hard to describe the effect of such a scene on a foreign witness. The red earth, the colourful garments — as though a child had gone mad with his paint box — the chattering monkeys high up in the trees, the heat — I must not forget the heat! — the pride on the face of the new parents (for the mother now had charge of the baby once his official promenade was over), the dignity of the old men. It was like an illustration in a book come to life.

We didn't stay long. Brodie drank some whiskey and munched on something that looked like dried grasshoppers; I drank from his flask and nibbled on some fresh coconut and then we left.

"Well?" said Brodie, as he escorted me back along the avenue to the Castle. "How did you like it?"

"I enjoyed everything about it but the spitting; I thought that was disgusting."

"It's necessary. Something to do with the child's *kra* or soul."

"I'm surprised he isn't dead the next day."

"A little drop of rum isn't going to hurt him."

"It's the way the rum was administered."

"One gets used to such things. It would be a terrible thing if that part of the ceremony were left out. These people have an elaborate belief system; it just doesn't happen to be ours. We take a baby to church, where some holy water is splashed on its head, at which point he or she is given a name. It's not so very different, is it?"

"The priest doesn't spit the holy water into the baby's mouth!"

"There is that. The Baptists go in for total immersion when a person is baptized, a complete dunking. That has always seemed quite extraordinary to me. I suppose it's following the tradition of John the Baptist."

George

ONE AFTERNOON, WHEN CRUICKSHANK was once again in Cape Coast, I heard him call her "Letty" as he was taking his leave. I wanted to shout down to him, "She's Mrs. Maclean to you, old chap," but of course I didn't.

I spoke to Letty about it instead.

"I heard Cruickshank call you 'Letty' this afternoon."

"That's my name."

"Did you tell him to do this?"

"Well, of course. He's become one of my best friends. Maybe my only friend."

"I think he should call you 'Mrs. Maclean,' like everybody else."

"Oh, pooh!"

"I think I shall have to speak to him."

"What are you going on about?"

"People talk."

"What people? What people are there to talk? Mr. Topp? Mr. Freeman? Mr. Swanzy? Mr. Hutton? Ibrahim?

"My reputation is important to me. This isn't London. I know you were used to having 'best friends' of the opposite sex back home, but it won't do here."

"What do you mean by that remark?"

"I simply mean that you should be less informal."

"Are you saying he shouldn't call on me when he comes to Cape Coast?"

"I'm saying he should call you 'Mrs. Maclean' and perhaps he shouldn't call on you quite so often."

Letty

I PUT DOWN MY KNIFE AND FORK and pushed my plate away.

"I do my domestic chores every morning: so much flour, so much sugar, so much tea. I plan the menu for the day and direct which rooms are to be cleaned. Then I retire to my own rooms to write. I work very hard, as I want to send some, if not all, of the Scott essays home with the October ship. It is solitary work and it occupies me fully in the mornings. I don't mind; I like it; it's what I do. And I don't mind eating my noon-day meal alone, as I am still thinking about my writing. But after that hours and hours go by before I see you at dinnertime. Even a siesta can only take up an hour or so. Mr. Cruickshank's visits have filled a void. He's very well-informed about the natives on this coast and I am learning about all sorts of things. Did you know that the women here give birth sitting on a special stool? That they are never to cry out, for that would be shameful."

"You talk about such things with Brodie Cruickshank?"

"He talks about such things; I listen."

"This is not proper!"

"I'm amazed; I truly am amazed. I am not in a position to sally forth and ask questions myself; that *would* be improper. But I am fascinated by the local customs and am taking notes with an eye to writing an article or two for the journals back home."

"On birthing stools."

"Perhaps not on birthing stools, but there are lots of other interesting things I could write about."

"Well I don't like it."

"Well I don't care whether you like it or not."

With that I rose from my chair and flounced out. "Proper/improper": my God! What a prig George was. Should I flounce back in and quiz him about his country wife, his "wench" — disgusting term. That's one of the "local customs," too. Proper for out here, of course, and anyway, he's a man. "Smacks of the barnyard, it does," pronounced Mrs. Bailey one day, when she was discussing this quaint custom.

"My sentiments exactly," I replied.

However, a half-hour's reflection made me realize I had handled this all wrong. What if he forbade Brodie to come again? I was so used, now, to our tête-à-têtes about anything and everything that I would be positively bereft without them. It was bad enough that he would be away for months and months, but I was steeling myself for that, and George had promised, as well, a visit to Accra over the Christmas holidays. (Little did he know I had a wonderful fruit-cake from Fortnum and Mason's, all wrapped up in rum-soaked cheesecloth and hidden in a tin. I intended to hold a little soirée on Christmas Eve.)

George was jealous; it was as simple as that. I hadn't thought he loved me enough to be jealous, but he was — jealous and possessive — and I must make haste to placate him.

The cover had been removed, but he was still sitting at the table, staring at his hands.

"George," I said, "I have come to apologize."

"And I must apologize to you. I never meant for you to spend so much time alone. My illness, the death of my secretary; I'm overwhelmed. Unfortunately I can't do anything about it just now, but things will get better, I promise"

"George, let's not quarrel anymore; it upsets us both." And I held out my hand. He rose from his chair, smiling.

"I'll tell you what," he said. "Would you like to come up to the cock-loft and look at the moon?"

He touched the back of my neck as he steadied the telescope for me. And there was the moon, the same moon that shone down upon London earlier. Full of craters, not smooth as it appears to the ordinary eye.

"This is magical," I said. "Thank you for bringing me here." And by here I meant not just to his sacred cockloft (he even dusted it himself), but here to Cape Coast.

I think I was more in love with him that night, than I ever was before or since.

George

I TOUCHED THE BACK OF HER NECK; her hair was put up because of the heat. If what I felt that night wasn't love, I don't know what it was.

"Let's go downstairs," I said. "Let us read together and then go to bed."

Brodie Cruickshank

I KNEW THERE WAS A LOCAL WEDDING about to take place and I asked Letty if she'd like to go. She accepted and said Mrs. Bailey would be coming along as well as she'd set her heart on seeing a "darkie wedding."

So I called for them a few days later, a little put out that I wasn't escorting Letty alone, but never mind, one can't always have everything one wants. Mrs. Bailey had on her church-going outfit, complete with straw bonnet, while Letty was in a frock of palest green, with a deeper green turban on her head. They had both, in their own ways, paid careful attention to their toilette.

Letty

AFTER THAT OUTDOORING CEREMONY I wasn't quite sure what to expect — would the groom spit in the bride's mouth and declare her his? Would they consult the entrails of a chicken to see how many "pikkins" they were likely to have?

I should not have been so cynical. Mr. Topp had offered us prime seats on his verandah, his wife not there because she was a female relation of the young girl and was busy dressing her for the occasion.

The procession advanced along the avenue, preceded by gong-gongs and drummers and the obligatory firing of muskets and then there was the girl with her attendants. She wore a rich blue silk skirt from her waist to her ankles and over it was some sort of padded bustle, held on by a broad silk scarf of brilliant yellow. Above the waist she was naked, but had been painted all over with fine lines of white clay, almost as though she were wearing a fitted blouse of delicate lace. There were gold ornaments in her hair and gold at ears, wrists, and ankles. She passed quite close to us and as she did, she turned her head slightly and smiled. It was the smile of a princess, a future queen. Brodie said later that he was often reminded of a young fawn or a beautiful colt when he saw these young girls decked out in all their (sometimes borrowed) finery. I could not help thinking of my own dull wedding in my plain grey dress, with only two attendants to stand up for us. Here all of the women in the town seemed to be involved, not just relations or close friends, and there was to be a communal feast later in the evening.

The girl could not have been more than fourteen, but they marry early here and are often betrothed long before they are of an age to marry.

"And if they do not care for their betrothed?" I asked.

"That presents complications and there are elaborate rules to cover such eventualities. People tend to think of the Africans as savages, and certainly there are cruel practices, and even cannibalism, among some tribes. But for the most part their lives are full of rituals that must be adhered to. If someone disobeys, there are punishments."

I asked Mrs. Bailey how she had liked the wedding procession.

"All right, I suppose, if you like that sort of thing."

"What sort of thing? Marriage?"

"Parading around half-naked. Showing herself off like that. No civilized woman would do that."

"It is the custom here."

"Yes. Well." (Sniff)

Yet she got on famously with Ibrahim and Isaac, with the women in the market. And she was teaching the group of little pra-pra girls how to knit. I tried to imagine Mrs. Bailey "parading around" naked or even half-naked. She had stopped wearing her stays unless she were leaving the Castle for some reason; as a result she was shapeless from shoulder to (I guess) knee and went around in a large garment of market cloth — magenta with big green circles on it. She resembled some large, at present undiscovered, animal, colourful cousin to the grey hippopotamus.

The drums go *Dá Da Da/Dá Da Da/Dá Da Da/Dá Da Da/Dá Da Da*; the sea flings itself against the shore; the hyrax screams in the coconut palms; the cockroaches fled to the corners when I retired to my room with a lamp. I hated the cockroaches; they were everywhere, even in my armoire. Sometimes they ran over my hands when I went to lift out a petticoat or a pair of stockings; I taught myself not to scream. I shook out my shoes every morning, in case of scorpions. When a sausage fly fell into the soup tureen, I watched as Isaac calmly fished it out with the ladle and threw it on the floor.

"I think if we all disappeared from Africa overnight," Brodie said, "the insects would take over."

One of the soldiers died from a snake bite; two more fishermen drowned.

"Well, Letty," said George, releasing his serviette from its ring, "Everything all right? Any complaints?"

I did not tell him I was having trouble sleeping when I retired to my own room at night. I did not tell him I was sure someone stood outside my door. Instead I listened to his stories of what the palaver had been that day: mortgages, pledges, property agreements, and pawns. All to be arbitrated by the Gubbner. A lends B his cutlass for a month because B says he needs it to cut down a bamboo tree; but B uses the cutlass to cut odum wood, which he proceeds to sell. A can claim his cutlass back before the end of the month *and* compel B to give compensation for the sale of the wood.

"It all sounds very tiresome."

"It would be, except that the Fantees are great orators, positive Romans when they get going. Imagine giving an impassioned speech over a torn shirt."

"Perhaps if it's your only one?"

"Perhaps. But I sometimes think the bit of rag is only an excuse for a heated debate. And they can be quite poetic. One of the standard retorts is: 'Bery good. Bery good. Me loose, me go for eat stones for chop.'"

"So you enjoy being Solomon?"

"In a way. But what I do is important, also. The natives have to learn that they will get a fair hearing if they come to me. They don't need to bribe petty chiefs or present gifts to receive what passes for justice here. Over the years I have built up quite a reputation for impartiality. They may go away grumbling if they lose the case, but they know I have examined it from all sides.

"However, we need the missionaries as well. I know you don't care for Thomas Freeman, but if the British are ever to rule here, Christianity must prevail and the old superstitions be discarded."

"Do you think that will happen?"

"I hope so; I wouldn't be out here if I didn't think it was important for us to establish ourselves on this coast. Not as slavers — that's over and done with — but as benevolent rulers, as Christian rulers, as kind, just men."

"What if they don't wish to be ruled?"

"They will have no choice. I do worry about the Ashantee — these people are kittens compared to the Ashantee. If we can subdue *them*, I think we shall prevail."

"And then?"

"Pardon?"

"What then? When they've been subdued?"

We went every Sunday to hear Mr. Freeman preach. As we strolled along the avenue the people smiled and dipped their heads. I think the men would have tugged at their forelocks if they'd had them.

Although the roof and windows were not yet installed in the new chapel, it held many more people and so Mr. Freeman chose to preach there. It also, he said, reminded him of the lay preachers who had stood in the open and preached to the country people back home. He drew inspiration from that thought.

I thought his sermons very clever; he adapted them to suit the people for whom they were intended. "Cut your coat to suit your cloth" as the old saying goes. Yam harvests came into it, fevers came into it, snakes came into it (of course). Lots of talk, also, about devils and false gods. Lots of references to Jesus-God and how He sacrificed Himself for You (pointing) and You (pointing) and Yes, even You (pointing to a little group of boys leaning in at the windows). The boys grinned, showing their bright white teeth.

He had a beautiful preaching voice and he could get quite worked up as he went on, dabbing at his forehead and lips with a big white handkerchief.

He spoke in English and then, Joseph, the most fluent of those already converted, translated all this into Fantee. He had told us one evening, when he came to dine, that after observing the power of the paramount chiefs, who spoke to the people only through a linguist, he had decided to adopt this principle for his preaching. He felt it gave him more power this way, and he even had the translator hold a mahogany stick with a cross carved onto the top.

When Mr. Freeman talked to me or conversed at the dinner table, he kept his voice soft and low. But when he preached! When he was filled with the spirit, how he boomed, how we seemed to be in the very presence of a God-drenched messenger. I always felt it was such a pity he had chosen as his interpreter Joseph Bannerman, a pleasant enough fellow, but with no fire. Mr. Freeman's sermons, when given in English, could stir even a cynic like myself, but Mr. Bannerman? Everything was presented in the same monotone, no great hills, no deep valleys, no triumphs or despairs. I hoped he would abandon this "linguist" idea (surely *he* was already the linguist and God the great chief or king?) and learn the Fantee language.

When I died, he was still anxiously awaiting word from the Wesley-an Committee about a new wife. I suggested to George that perhaps he should order two, since the mortality amongst missionary wives was so high.

"Or why stop at two? Why not half a dozen? Like ladies-in-waiting."

George: "I will pretend I didn't hear that." (But I could see he was suppressing a smile.)

The Castle band sometimes helped out with the hymns. Mr. Free-man would sing a line in his nice baritone; we would all repeat it; then another line, repeat; another, and so on.

> An-chent of Days
> (An-chent of Days)
> Who sit — ethroned in Glo-ree

The band also played in front of the Castle on Sunday afternoons. They were mostly very old men in very old castoff uniforms. Why was I surprised that their repertoire consisted mostly of old Jacobite airs? A large and appreciative crowd usually collected for this performance. The old trumpeter received the most applause when he performed one of his solos.

Mrs. Topp had her baby, a boy, William Kofee. There was an outdooring as well as a christening; George and I were asked to be godparents, and from somewhere George produced a silver christening cup. (Later he said it had been left behind years ago, when a Mrs. Bowdich, who had lived at the Castle, lost her infant daughter.) Mrs. Bailey, who was always knitting, produced an entire layette, more suitable perhaps for a temperate clime, but very impressive. I had nothing to give but my blessing and some castile soap. I made a note to send for something with the next boat.

George

I WAS DELIGHTED FOR THE TOPPS — a big, strong, healthy boy. I was also a little envious.

Mr. Freeman

I WAS DELIGHTED FOR THE TOPPS, although I was not too happy that Mrs. Topp, a good Christian, insisted on the outdooring ceremony. I must admit I was also a little envious of their happiness.

Brodie Cruickshank

I WAS SO PLEASED THAT EVERYTHING had gone right. Now if the child could manage to get through the first year without dying of some fever or another. It made me realize once again that it was high time I took me a wife.

Letty

DID SHE CRY OUT? Did her suffering Christian self get the better of her more traditional self? I screamed and screamed; the pain was red-hot; the flames of Hell would be nothing compared to it.

Mrs. Bailey would insist on telling me all about "our Dulcie" and how she had "woke up the whole neighbourhood." And yet our Dulcie was expecting another; how could she? Mrs. Bailey hoped she would be back home in time for the confinement; she was already knee-deep in little knitted soakers.

"There's something about new life, isn't there, Mrs. Maclean, that makes it all seem worthwhile."

Clack. Clack. Clack. As she turned the heels on another pair of wee booties.

"Ibrahim," I said, "one of the children left this doll outside my door. Would you know whose it is? They aren't supposed to come up to our apartments unless invited, but I shouldn't like the child to get into trouble."

When he turned around to look at what I was holding out, he uttered a cry, snatched it from me, and threw it on the fire.

"Why, what did you do that for?"

He was shaking all over, and muttering.

"What are you saying?"

"No good, Madame. She no good a-tall."

"George," I said that evening, "something peculiar happened today."

George

I DIDN'T WANT TO FRIGHTEN HER so I laughed it off, but from then on I had Isaac move his sleeping mat up to the top of the stairs. He was very reluctant to do so — no doubt Ibrahim had told him about the doll, but I insisted. And then I went to make some inquiries down in the town. The gates were opened at 5:00 a.m. every morning and closed at 8:00 p.m. each night unless we were entertaining. The keys were always brought to me at 9:00 p.m. And yet I couldn't believe this doll had been placed there by any of the soldiers or servants. I put the word out; if any *ju-ju* of any sort was found within the Castle grounds, I, personally, would find out the perpetrator and throw him in prison for "long time." I said "him," but I wondered.

Letty

MR. FREEMAN CALLED ON ME about once a week, usually just to report on how well things were going with the mission. He had brought out yards of black gabardine and white calico and as the people converted and declared themselves for Jesus and the one true God, he had pants and shirts made up for the boys and men, skirts and blouses for the girls and women.

"To set them apart, you know. And each receives a badge to go on the pocket over the heart."

"Is this not a bribe — the new outfit, the badge?"

"How so? They must first complete their studies and submit to baptism. Only then will they receive their new clothes. They will stand apart; they will look smart."

"And others will be impressed."

"That is my hope."

(I thought the black-and-white theme made Christianity look rather dull. This was a people who loved colour.)

"They will also receive a Bible, and in it will be written their name, the date of their baptism and my signature."

"The Bible is full of difficult words; will they be able to read it?"

"Not at first, perhaps not for many years. But they will know it contains the Word of God. That is enough for the present."

"They will like the stories," I said. "The Bible is full of good stories."

He cleared his throat. "Dare I ask you, once again, if you would be willing to help out?"

"You may ask, but my answer will be the same. I'm afraid I'm too busy just now. Perhaps later on."

Mr. Freeman: Too busy talking about novels and poetry to Brodie Cruickshank.

Letty: Why couldn't I spare an hour or two a week to teach the little savages? Get one of the carvers to make a set of wooden letters: *A* is for Africa, *B* is for Bamboo, *C* is for Castle, *D* is for … what could *D* be for? *D* is for Don't Want to Do it.

"Doesn't it bother you," Mr. Freeman said, "living in the Castle?"

"Actually, it's very comfortable. George has done everything possible to ensure that that is so. I was quite surprised and delighted when I saw our quarters."

"Do you know why these castles and forts were built, Mrs. Maclean? Cape Coast, Elmina, Anamaboe, Dixcove … ?"

"Of course I do."

"And it doesn't bother you to live in such a place?"

"All that is ancient history."

"Really? Five years is 'ancient history'?"

"There has been no slave-trading here for a long time."

"Hmm. Have you been down to the dungeons, Mrs. Maclean?"

"No."

"Men like my father, who was only a boy at the time, were captured in the Interior, shackled together, and marched down here or to places like this. People who had never seen the sea. Terrified. Separated from family and home. Crammed into rooms — no, cells — with little ventilation, so many together that often they slept standing up. Do you know what the floor of those cells is paved with, Mrs. Maclean? You have a lively imagination; use it."

"Why are you telling me all this?"

"Because you need to know, you who are so enamoured of the picturesque. Picture this, Mrs. Maclean. Maybe one hundred people crammed into a cell eight feet by ten feet, or even smaller. Taken out into the sunlight once a day to be sluiced down by their jailors. The sunlight, Mrs. Maclean. You know how it makes us blink, how you yourself cannot go out in it without your parasol. Imagine how their eyes felt — that sudden glare! And then shut up in the almost-darkness once again.

"You know what they did, sometimes, with the strongest men? They hung them upside down to weaken them a bit, to make sure they didn't start anything. And then, finally, they were taken out and led single-file through what the abolitionists called 'The Door of No Return.' Shoved into canoes, hauled on deck the slave ships, tossed into the hold. Men, women, children. Nobody will ever know how many, Mrs. Maclean; good records were not kept. Thousands and thousands at any rate. Shipped to the plantations of the New World. If they died en route, they were tossed overboard. 'Full fathom five …' Oh yes, I know my Shakespeare. I sometimes think that is why the sea is so relentless here. It's the bones of all those dead Africans, stirring things up. Hoping the castles and forts will tumble down.

"My father was taken to Jamaica, where he worked for years, first cutting cane and then in the rendering huts, stripped to the waist in temperatures no human being should ever have to endure. But then, slaves weren't human beings, were they? Fall behind at all and you were whipped. My father's back was covered in raised scars; he was a gardener, as I became, but he never took his shirt and jacket off even on the hottest day. If I think about what they did to my father my faith wavers. But it is not for me to question the ways of God. There has to be a reason for all that horror, and some day it will become clear. All that so you could put sugar in your tea!"

"I think you should go now, Mr. Freeman."

"And I think you should make a visit to the cells. Don't go at night; hundreds of bats fly around down there. Some say they are the souls of those who were confined there. Who knows?"

Letty

I DID NOT LOOK AT HIM. How dare he tell me all this? I never owned a slave; no one in my family ever owned a slave. Of course it was horrible, but what could I do to make it better?

At the door, he turned.

"I'll leave you to think on these things, Mrs. Maclean. The floors of those cells are still paved with layer upon layer of human excrement. Good day."

It was shortly after that when I began to feel unwell.

He sent a little note around the next day, with some garden eggs and green beans from his garden. He apologized for perhaps "going too far." After all, he could not afford to lose George Maclean's good will and he did enjoy the dinners at the Castle. He said he got carried away. I did not reply to his note, but neither did I mention the incident to George.

Brodie Cruickshank

I HAD A GREAT DEAL OF BUSINESS to get through at Anamaboe and so I didn't see Letty for several days. When I finally returned to Cape Coast, she seemed very subdued.

"Is something troubling you?"

"I don't sleep through the night. And I have bad dreams."

"It sounds to me as though you have a touch of fever. Why don't you get the surgeon to have a look at you?"

"No. No. I'm fine. It's just that it's so noisy here at night."

"Isn't London noisy at night?"

"Not where I live … lived! Very quiet. And I tended to write very late at night, in London, after I'd been out for an evening. Here we go to bed quite early — or I do. I'm not sure when George actually sleeps."

"Are the essays going well?"

"Oh yes. There are no worries on that score."

"Would you read to me?"

"I'd be delighted. I've missed our afternoons. Perhaps I'm just a bit melancholy as I know they are drawing to an end."

I was amazed at how much she had accomplished in just a few short weeks. Each woman was described so precisely I could actually *see* them. The essays were thoughtful, philosophical. It was almost as though she had the uncanny ability to look into Scott's brain and clearly see his intentions. The women were the most interesting; they were the focus of the book, after all, but the men were interesting, too. Her humour is evident throughout:

> It is no paradox to say that the country is never so
> much enjoyed as by the dwellers in cities. How
> many there are who live eleven months on the hope

of the twelfth given to some brief and delightful wandering. Even in the dull and mindless routine of a watering place, where shrimps and gossip are the Alpha and Omega of the day, there is refreshment and relief …

I was simply dazzled by these little portraits.

"If you were just starting out, Letty, these essays would make your name. As it is, they will make your star shine even brighter."

"Do you really think so?"

"I do."

She remained thoughtful for a few minutes and I was about to take my leave when she said, "The other day Mr. Freeman suggested I should re-read *Robinson Crusoe*. I said I had reread it many times, but he just smiled and shook his head."

"Had you been discussing shipwrecks, perhaps, or self-reliance?"

"No, nothing like that. We were 'discussing,' or rather, he was delivering a harangue about the slave trade. I found it most offensive. What has Robinson Crusoe to do with the slave trade?"

"I begin to see what he was getting at; Crusoe was heavily involved in the slave trade."

"Surely not!"

"Yes. He was. That's how he got the money that his friends put by for him when he was lost."

"I didn't notice that."

"Why would you? You probably didn't even think about slavery. Few who weren't involved in it, or abolitionists, gave it a second thought."

"And the Europeans on this coast?"

"Well of course they thought about it. They not only held slaves, they also supplied stores to the slaving ships."

"Did you do that?"

"No, it was pretty well all over when I arrived. Although Anamaboe

Fort held many slaves in its heyday."

"Did George have anything to do with slaves?"

"The Council here was not allowed to trade. In anything. If ships stood out in the roads and sent for supplies, he could hardly refuse to sell them what they needed, but he couldn't very well go out and inspect the ships himself."

"Does any slave-trading still go on?"

"I expect so. One hears rumours. You see, it was considered acceptable for such a long time and was such a lucrative business; there are many of the old traders who refuse to honour laws that are made across the sea."

"If they are caught?"

"If they are caught, they face enormous fines, and the slaves are freed. We have to find other ways for men to make money on this coast. Palm oil is one, and we'll find others."

"Others as lucrative as selling people?"

"Letty," I said, "times change. We used to exhibit the heads of criminals on pikes. We still enjoy hangings and bear-baitings and earlier than that we used to run around nearly naked and covered in blue grease — or the Welsh did, at any rate. Kings beheaded wives they wanted to get rid of. As civilization progresses, things that seemed perfectly acceptable at one time become unacceptable later on."

"I know Mr. Freeman is counting on that. Wants to do away with all those fetishes and multiple gods."

"I'm not sure the Wesleyans are going about it the right way. A little less of the 'Thou shalt not' might help."

"How many slaves do you think went from here to the New World? Mr. Freeman implied thousands."

"A steady stream at any rate. It's over now, Letty; there's nothing you can do about it."

I left her looking even more pensive than when I arrived.

Letty

THUNDER, BUT NO RAIN. Thunder and great streaks of lightning, but no rain. Then, suddenly, the rain would come, falling straight down and galloping across the roofs like a pack of wild horses. The red earth turned to red mud, red pudding. Then, just as suddenly, it was over. Everything steamed. The earth sucked up the wet.

It rained the afternoon I was buried. George stayed in his room.

The Castle gun was fired at 8:00 p.m., just before the heavy gates were closed. The keys were brought to George at 9:00 p.m. No one could get in or out from the closing of the gates until they opened the following morning.

Isaac now slept at the top of the stairs, yet someone stood outside my door, breathing, waiting. Someone left me another doll, just two sticks tied together with red cloth and a flat piece of wood for the head. Something a child would make. Or maybe not. I told no one; I locked it in my secret drawer.

They said the bats that flew around the lowest level of the Castle were the souls of slaves. These are a superstitious people; Mr. Freeman is out to change all that.

When Mr. Freeman got his congregation really worked up they jumped up and down and shouted. He held up his hands, palms outward.

"Quiet now. Quiet. Let us pray."

When he called to see me, I sent word that I was busy, perhaps another time. Always he left a note and a little gift from his garden, some flowers.

I longed for letters and journals and newspapers, but consoled myself with the thought the *Maclean* would soon be in. October, now, and back home, the loveliest time of the year. "Season of mists and mellow fruitfulness." My friends would be returning to Town from their country homes. There would be parties and new fashions. New faces. George said we could go to Accra during the Christmas holidays. Two days to get there, two days to come back. Brodie told me the officers dance with one another — the Dashing White Sergeant, Eightsome Reels, Minuets, even.

"You will be the belle of the ball."

"I am not a natural dancer; I can't seem to concentrate on the steps. Too many things going on at once. I'm all for sitting on a little gilded chair with a glass of punch and watching."

"I think you are just being modest."

Mrs. Bailey, my plump Abigail, would be leaving with the ship. I told her I planned a party for Christmas Eve and would she teach Ibrahim to make mince pies?

"Don't know what we can use for suet."

"Just do your best with what we've got in the stores. I know there are raisins and of course there's plenty of brandy."

"I suppose I could candy some peel."

"There, you see; I knew you'd be able to help. Perhaps, if you made up a great stock of the filling, using brandy to preserve it, and you taught him the pastry, he would have no trouble putting it all together." Anything to do with sweets and Mrs. Bailey was interested. (And I had several tins of Scotch shortbread if all else failed.) I wished we could have oysters as a first course, but it didn't really matter; when in Rome … There were snails in the market, Isaac said, but they were dismissed by Mrs. B. as "revolting" and "huge." I was hoping for *escargot*.

New books, new faces, new topics of conversation. Here it is always the climate, the natives, who is dying, who dead. And the sea never stops; there is just a pause, a moment of unbearable tension, then *WHAM!* it begins again.

The wind in the palm trees rattles the leaves like bones.

Brodie Cruickshank

I SUPPOSE I WAS A LITTLE IN LOVE WITH HER. At any rate I loved everything about her that was familiar and feminine, English and civilized. I considered George Maclean a very lucky man.

Letty

PERHAPS SOMEDAY SOMEONE WILL WRITE A SAD BALLAD about all this, something along the lines of Barbara Allen or Lord Randall. George could have it set to music and play it on his violin.

George

SOMETIMES I THOUGHT OF HOME, but not too often; as I told Letty, it is not good to live in two places at once. The most successful men, out here, are those who arrive with the idea they will stay forever — except for the occasional leave for reasons of health. And yet and yet. I imagined the snow on the hilltops after the first frosts in September. The rain and fog would seem to go on forever and then along would come one clear crisp blue day to make up for all the rest.

I missed the sound of the cuckoo on the moors in spring, finding the nests of the curlew in the heather, the drumming of the male snipe. All the birds — there were so many birds. Land birds, sea birds. Here the most prominent bird is the vulture. He is always up there, wheeling in great circles, looking for something dead or dying. "Nature's dustman."

"Did you know, Letty, that Macbeth was one of us?"

"I knew he was a Scot."

"He was a Scot from my area, a Mormoir, or sea stewart, who headed the Celtic resistance to the encroachments of a new regime and the new language that followed."

"Macbeth was a very bad man."

"A weak man, an ambitious man — or at least that is how Shakespeare portrayed him; his wife was the bad one."

"Shakespeare's women are so various. Viola is my favourite. Perhaps, when I finish the Scott essays, I should turn to Shakespeare."

"Not another novel?"

"Not at present. *Ethel Churchill* wore me out. And I must admit that it is much harder for me to write prose than poetry. Poetry seems my native language; it just flies off my pen. Whereas prose — prose is like a foreign language to me."

"The essays are in prose."

"But that is different. I am operating as a critic there; I am not the prime mover."

"I admire your self-discipline."

"It was something I learned at a very early age. And then, since my early twenties, I have always been aware of the wolf at the door. I did not write solely for pleasure; I still don't. I write to feed the wolf."

George

I HAD A FEELING that when the boat came in, Letty might feel a great tug toward "Home." That is why I agreed to the Accra expedition at Christmas. I would much prefer to stay here, sleep late, catch up on all my work, but she needed something to look forward to. Unless the Wesleyan Society was sending out more missionaries with this ship, once Mrs. Bailey left, Letty would be the only white woman here. And she absolutely refused to get involved with the Mission School; she seemed to have taken a positive dislike to Mr. Freeman when she could have been such a help to him. I would never force her to do anything, but it did look peculiar when the little school was so badly in need of teachers. I didn't think it was because he was a mulatto; it was something deeper than that. And certainly there was a time later on when I disliked him heartily. It was a misunderstanding, but it cost me dear.

Letty: George, if he says "Adam's Ale" once more I shall scream!

Letty (to Brodie): A horse in a mill has an easier life than an author.

Mr. Freeman (raising his voice): "My chains fell off, my heart was free; I rose, went forth and followed Thee." (He paused to make sure his linguist understood and could translate properly.)
   "Did you get all that?"
   "Sah."

Letty (Mr. Freeman and several others are dining at the Castle): "Perhaps you should take a native wife this time, Mr. Freeman, as the climate does not seem to suit these European ladies."
   "It seems to suit *you*, Mrs. Maclean."
   "Yes, it does. Much to my surprise. I haven't felt so well in months."

"Not even a hint of fever?"
"Not a hint, not a whisper."
"God is smiling down on you, dear lady."
"So it would seem."

Letty

THE CLEANERS FOUND A DEAD BAT under my bed. "Isaac," I called to the breathing outside my door, "is that you?"

I began to slow down with my writing of the essays. I knew I would finish in time to send them off, but I was unsure of what to do after that. I was contracted to do the next year's *Drawing-Room Scrapbook* and the engravings should arrive with the boat, but I could do three dozen poems to go with three dozen engravings in the twinkling of an eye. Then what? Perhaps I should begin a novel, something to keep my mind from my night terrors. There was the story Brodie had told me about that governor of Elmina, of how, if the women he chose became pregnant, they were set free. A young girl from the interior is walked down to the Coast with her brother and a hundred others. They are locked in the cells and only taken out when the slave traders arrived, or to have their daily airing in the courtyard. The governor, from his balcony, looked down on the naked women from above. "My" girl is very lovely, like the bride we saw in the wedding procession, and of course she is chosen.

Pointing. "That one. Yah. Her."

How would the other women feel when it is discovered she is with child? Would they be envious — now she wouldn't have to board a slaving ship to be transported God knows where? Or would they feel deeply sorry for her, knowing the brutal reputation of the governor, knowing that this had been her first time with a man?

At four months, her condition is evident and the jailers make their report. The governor would quite like to keep her with him — she is so young and beautiful, like a young antelope, but a rule is a rule and he considers himself an honourable man.

When the great gates are shut behind her she stands frozen to the spot. Where can she go? What should she do? She stares up at the indifferent stars, her beautiful eyes full of tears. She has not even been allowed to say goodbye to her brother. All she can do is stumble away from the Castle toward the fires of the little town, terrified that some wild animal will spring from the shadows and catch her in its jaws. (There must be a bit of moonlight, but not much.)

As to what might happen after that, I wasn't sure. Would she give birth to a boy or a girl? Would she be befriended by a market woman, a merchant's wife, a degenerate trader? I would like her to have a happy ending, but I fear that won't be her fate. Perhaps her daughter will have the happy ending, or her son. Maybe the missionaries will take her in. (Would there have been missionaries at Elmina at that time? Brodie would know.)

It could have been a very good novel. The crashing surf, the Dutch governor, the terrified girl climbing the ladder to his quarters. Palm trees. Monkeys. Perhaps one of those awful "ordeals" Mrs. Topp mentioned, to establish guilt or innocence. The Southern Cross. The slave traders who stand in a little room with a peephole, so that they can see the slaves but cannot be seen themselves. "That one."

Her brother has to come into it — his story. He ends up in Jamaica, working in the cane fields. Three volumes.

"By Letitia Maclean, formerly L.E.L."

I lay on my bed in the afternoons, watching the dimity curtains billow in the breeze from the sea. If *Ethel Churchill* brought in £300, why shouldn't this bring in more? I would call it, *The Desolate Shore*.

"Brodie," I said, "tell me more about the days of the slave trade."

"What do you want to know?"

It got hotter every day now and I found I had little appetite. My old pain returned, but I rationed the drops carefully; they had to last. George was so caught up in Castle business he never noticed how listlessly I pushed the food around my plate. I had terrible dreams, but when I awoke, shaking and sweaty, I could not remember them. Mrs. Bailey began going through her trunk to see what she could leave behind. There had to be room for the mountains of knitted goods she was taking home to our Dulcie.

"Are you looking forward to leaving, Mrs. Bailey?"

"I'm not looking forward to the voyage; I expect I shall be sick the whole way across, but I'm looking forward to being back in England. This has all been very interesting and I've certainly been treated well, but it's not home, is it? Colourful though, innit? So different. Out of the ordinary. I certainly never thought I'd have a chance to see Africa, did you? Funny where life takes you."

It was Mrs. Bailey who closed my eyes and dressed me in my prettiest blue-sprigged frock. "Laid me out," as they say. George sat in his room with his head in his hands. Mrs. Bailey said George should come and remove my rings as they were his mother's, but he refused. I don't think he wanted to touch me.

George: She was so cold, so still.

Mr. Freeman

THE HEAT AFFECTED ME — HOW COULD IT NOT? — but what really plagued me were the flying insects, especially the mosquitoes; they always seemed to head for my ears, which are rather large and fleshy. I lay there sleepless, for a month, until I devised a kind of canopy from the net curtains my wife had brought with her. After that I slept as sound as a newborn babe. The other men laughed at me, I know, and my cook-steward grinned in a mocking manner, but I tell you, my canopy, plus cotton-wool ear plugs against that awful whine, well, this changed my whole perception of the place.

There were skeps at Sir Robert Harland's and I got the idea for my canopy from the hats with nets hanging down, that we used when collecting honey from the supers. Of course the sting of a bee is much more painful than that from a mosquito, but I am a practical man and like to find solutions for problems. If the mosquitoes were depriving me of my sleep, then I must find a way to correct that.

I wondered if it would be possible to keep bees out here. My garden grew well and my aubergines were fat and glossy, my beans plentiful, my onions excellent. I had brought along some cuttings of herbs and medicinal plants as well, such as comfrey and sage, feverfew, and St. John's Wort. By the time Mrs. Maclean arrived I felt I could "show off" my little plot and she was very impressed.

I saw her once before, you know, even spoke to her, although of course she didn't remember me. She was one of a large house party that weekend and while wandering around the estate, seeking inspiration for a poem, no doubt, perhaps looking for the family mausoleum, she came across one of Sir Robert's granddaughters crying bitterly. It was not my job to attend to guests, except to supply nosegays for their rooms and perhaps bunches of grapes from the conservatory. The child didn't sound in danger or of course I would have gone to her aid — I was deadheading roses just around the corner.

Mrs. Maclean — Miss Landon as she was then — discovered what the trouble was, came looking for help, and saw me.

"You!" she called. "Miss Caroline's ball has fallen in the pond. Please fetch it for her."

She turned her back and expected me to follow. I brought with me my long rake and it proved an easy matter just to lean out over the pond and rake it in. Never a thank-you from either of them and the child put her hands behind her back.

"I don't want it now, it's all nasty."

I left it there on the lawn for somebody else to find and went back to the roses.

Miss High and Mighty. It's the ones without much money who are the worst. Sir Robert and Lady H. never used that tone with me, or with any of the servants, even if he did make me choose once I had seen the light. They didn't like Methodists? Well, few did.

Sir Robert said that he wished me well in whatever I did in future and shook my hand. (Of course at that point he didn't know I was going to take his housekeeper away as well!)

Letty

IT WAS HARD TO BELIEVE THAT THE MOON up there was the same moon that shines down on London. Did they talk about me? Did they sigh and say how dull London seemed now that Letty's gone?

Some nights, if I leant over the battlements, I could see the moon broken up into splinters, like a dropped plate, yet up in the sky it was whole. The night before I died, the moon was barely there, and then it disappeared altogether behind a build-up of cloud and mist.

"'There's husbandry in Heaven; their candles are all out.' Who says that? Banquo, is it, just before the murderers spring upon him?"

"I'm not sure," Brodie said. "You know your Shakespeare far better than I."

"I used to sit with my grandmother Bishop on a Sunday afternoon, and while she nodded over her tatting, I memorized page after page of Shakespeare. I do believe there is a line from the Bard to fit every occasion."

"'Parting is such sweet sorrow'?"

I shivered. "No, not that one; it's not really appropriate."

"Sorry. It just popped into my head."

He took out a little box he'd been keeping in his pocket.

"I have a present for you."

I turned away from him, once again staring out towards sea.

"You mustn't give me presents," I said.

"Just a keepsake to remember me by. Something curious. Hold out your hand. I had intended giving it to you in the morning, but there might not be an appropriate time."

"I can't imagine what it could be," I said, opening the box.

Inside was a little bird of brass, about the size of a man's thumb, quite beautifully done, with its head facing backwards.

"Do you know anything about 'lost wax'?" he asked.

"Only the thousands of candles I have consumed, writing at night, both in London and out here."

He smiled. "Lost wax is a very old process used by the Africans for making small objects, beads, for example, or gold weights. *Cire perdue.*"

"But this isn't gold; it's brass."

"True. But the gold weights — little brass figures of various design — are used to weigh small amounts of gold dust. All of the weights have numerical values. That's interesting in itself, but the main interest, for me, is that many of the weights have proverbs attached to them."

"And the bird with his head facing backwards, what does he mean?"

"I suppose the closest translation would be 'Had I known.'"

"Had I known what? Is this a message for me?"

"Not really. I just thought it was a fine example of the craft. I collect these. When I return I'll bring over some of them to show you, and if George is agreeable, I'll take you to a village where they do the casting."

"And if your wife is agreeable…"

"Don't be so sure that I'll return with a wife."

"You will — you will, and that will change everything."

Brodie: She turned it over and over in her hand, then put it in her little net bag.

"I shall treasure it. Just the name, 'Lost Wax,' gives it a kind of mystery. This is very sweet of you."

Letty: I locked it in my secret drawer. George never thought to look there when he sent the desk back to England. Never found the dolls, the little bat, the lump of clay with three feathers sticking into it. Did those things really have any power over me or did I give them that power? Certainly somebody was trying to frighten me. For the last few weeks I started at every sudden noise, couldn't sleep, could barely eat; the soup tasted strange; the chicken was a little 'off.' Were they trying to poison me as well?

Mrs. Bailey: I suppose I should have gone to her, insisted she tell me what was wrong, but it wasn't my place, was it. Any road, I figured it out for myself one day. After she died, when I was finished laying her out — she did look lovely — I leant down and whispered, "Don't worry, dear, your secret's safe with me."

Letty: I had always been good at masking my real feelings; George didn't notice a thing — except to comment from time to time on how "bonny" I looked.

"The *Maclean* will be here any day, Letty," George said. "Be sure to give me all your letters and I'll seal them in one packet addressed to Forster or your brother or whomever you wish. It will be easier that way."

"And my essays?"

"We'll seal those up in the same manner. I assume they go to William Jerdan?"

"He can deal with the publishing side, yes."

"The sooner you can hand me all this, the sooner I can see that it's packaged properly."

Letty: I handed over everything I had written to that date; but with the ship in, standing off in the roads but not yet ready to depart, I kept on writing letters. I wrote almost up until the moment of my death.

George: She never sealed her letters without showing them to me first. When the gossip-mongers began their malicious campaign it infuriated me. *Because* I saw her letters, she often teased me through them — it was a joke between us.

"There, George," she would say, "do you think I have blackened your character enough?" It was in jest.

Mrs. Bailey: One afternoon Mrs. Maclean swooned just after we came in. Swooned and vomited. She said it must have been the fish at luncheon. *Well, Emily,* I said to myself, *no good wondering about things that are none of your business.*

"Too much sun, mebbe," says I.

Letty

SOME THOUGHT I MODELLED MY DISCUSSION of Colonel Mannering on George, read things into that little essay that I never intended.

> The habits of a man accustomed to command —
> especially on a foreign station, would necessarily
> be removed and secluded. Now, what is but nec-
> essary authority in official life, and with man over
> man, seems harshness when extended to woman.

But I didn't invent Colonel Mannering; Scott did. And George was never harsh with me; he simply wasn't *there*. He knew I was occupied with my writing; he assumed I lacked for nothing (nothing material, that is), and so he was content.

In the mornings, as I worked, I could hear the voices of the prisoners who were sweeping and cleaning. Because I could not understand a word of what they were saying, it became nothing but sound and not in the least distracting. There seemed to be a lot of joking between the soldiers and their charges. I doubt those bayonets were ever used.

The vowels are rounder, very rich, although the women's voices, down in the town, are higher and more nasal.

The fishermen were the only men I noticed doing hard physical labour day after day (except Tuesdays, of course). It is the women who were constantly in motion, while the men stood around talking or sat under a silk-cotton tree playing Oware. A few men have special skills — the weavers, the carpenters, the drummers — but the universal skill seems to be avoiding work. I suppose if you have several wives, most of your needs are taken care of. George worked harder than ten of them put together; it was completely up to him to keep

order. The other members of the Council helped, Mr. Cobbold and
Mr. Topp in particular, yet no one seemed to have that keen sense of
duty that permeated my husband through and through. I wondered if
any of *them*, with a price upon their heads, would have gone alone to
confront the King of Apollonia?

Of course there was Mr. Freeman and he did work hard, but somehow that was different. Was it because he always let you know how
hard he worked?

"Ah, Mrs. Maclean! Now that the rains have virtually ceased, you
must come and see the progress we are making on the Chapel. I work
right alongside the men; I think that inspires them. In the heat of the
day we stop and share a simple meal of stew and fou-fou and then,
after an hour, we are up again and pounding away. The windows are
in and the men refused to take any money. Truly, I am blessed in my
endeavours!"

Me: C for Chapel; D for Drum; F for Fisherman; G for Goat.

Mr. Freeman: I often wished she would stop by and see me there,
stripped to the waist, see the strength in my back, my arms, admire
me. "Vanity, vanity." We all have our moments.

"Roof nearly on!" he called out to me as Mrs. Bailey and I made our
way to call on Mrs. Topp and the baby.

"Wonderful, Mr. Freeman," I called back. (But wouldn't you think
they'd put the roof on before putting in the windows?)

One day he did make a formal call, and, as I'd put him off several
times and Brodie was back at Anamaboe, I told Isaac to send him up.

"Ah, Mrs. Maclean. I just had to show you this. I am hoping it will be
the first of many such things to decorate the Children's Room."

It was a Noah's Ark, perhaps a foot long and a foot high, wonder-
fully carved, with all the pairs of animals you might find in Western

Africa — antelopes, monkeys, goats, snakes, parrots, crocodiles, pigs, elephants. And Mr. and Mrs. Noah, of course, dressed respectably (trousers and shirt for Mr. N., colourful dress with bodice and full sleeves for Mrs. N.).

"But what's this?" I said.

"What's what?"

"Mr. and Mrs. Noah have been painted white. Did the carver do that?"

"No," he said.

"Where is Mount Ararat, Mr. Freeman? Wouldn't Noah and his wife have been, at the very least, swarthy?"

"I need to emphasize the fact that they are of a different order than the Africans."

"I don't follow your thinking."

"That's all right; I brought the Ark here to be admired, not criticized."

"I do admire it; the carvings are wonderful. I'm just not sure you should 'Europeanize' the humans."

He went away shortly thereafter. Mr. Noah wore a hat and Mrs. Noah a bonnet, but the carver had given them recognizably African features. (Underneath hat and bonnet they probably sported woolly wooden hair.) I didn't point out to Mr. Freeman that he had forgotten to whiten their wrists and hands. What would he do to Moses or the disciples? I shuddered to think. When I told George about it that night, even he, who is very lenient towards Mr. Freeman, thought it was bizarre.

"What do you think he will do with Jesus?"

"These are Methodists, Letty. I doubt if there will be a crucifix anywhere, white or black."

A for Ark, then. *S* for Snake, the only letter that looks like what it represents. *F* for fever. *W* for Wench.

All the members of the Council had country wives, with the exception of Mr. Topp, so when George and I dined at their houses (which were very nice, white with green shutters, quite spacious and cool), I was the only lady present. When George had his country wife, did he take her with him, or did she remain back in the Castle, sulking? Did she ever *live* in the Castle? There were so many questions I couldn't ask.

When an officer dies here, it has been the custom to sell his clothes to other officers, partly to pay off any debts, partly because clothes, like everything else out here, deteriorate so quickly, and this way an officer could get new boots or a new shirt or breeches. However, Mrs. Bailey said a few things end up in the market and at the moment there was a quantity of clothes from the missionaries who had died. They did not have the same cachet as the things from the Castle, but still, they would gradually be purchased simply because they were European. Isaac told her that when a bundle of European clothes came into the market, it was called *Bronie wawu*: "a white man has died."

Why do these people set such store on the worn-out clothes of dead Europeans? George said the chiefs often ask for military garb (new) when they are trading. Tunics, boots (which they have to cut open because their feet are so wide), even cocked hats!

I don't blame the natives for turning up their noses at the missionaries' clothes, particularly the women. Who would want to go around dressed like a piece of old pewter?

I wonder what George did with my wardrobe? Did Mrs. Bailey pack it up and take the trunk to England when she finally left? Poor Mrs. Bailey. George asked her and Mr. Bailey, who had returned with the ship, to stay on for a bit. She must have missed "our Dulcie's" confinement. Perhaps she prevailed upon Brodie to carry the knitting back to London? She wasn't a bad sort, Mrs. Bailey, just not my sort. She did cause a lot of bother re: that bottle.

Every time I thought I was becoming accustomed to all the insect life and the general strangeness of the flora and fauna, something new came along.

I was just coming out of my room one morning when Mrs. Bailey's screams brought me running. I'm ashamed to say the first thing I thought of was that dreadful woman's warning in Eastbourne. Mrs. Bailey was being murdered by one of the servants or a desperate prisoner who had escaped. What had actually happened was this: she was unpinning our garments when the pole she used to adjust the line began to move. A python had curled itself around the pole — huge, maybe seven feet long. One of the soldiers ran it through with his bayonet and Ibrahim skinned it. I told him he could have the meat, we didn't want it, but to give half to the soldier.

Mrs. Bailey is shortsighted; she had to lie down for the rest of the afternoon. Later, I could hear laughter from the servants' quarters; I suppose they were delighting in the tale of the python and the washing pole, but that snake was enormous, something out of a nightmare, and she actually touched it, felt it move.

George went down to admire the skin, which was tacked up, drying, in the kitchen. Pythons have been known to kill a small goat, even a small child. God must have thought up some of these creatures when He was in a playful mood.

I told Brodie about Mr. Freeman and the Noah's Ark.

"He will go far, I think."

"Oh, Letty, you are wicked to make fun of him; he's very dedicated. He helps with the building of the chapel, right along with the other men."

"He believes he is one of those people destined to set the world right."

"Couldn't one say that about your husband?"

"No, never. He is not puffed up like Mr. Freeman. He simply tries to do his job as best he can."

"And Mr. Freeman is not doing that?"

"Mr. Freeman is doing his job for the glory of Mr. Freeman."

Brodie did agree that the black trousers and skirts, the white blouses and shirts, were probably a mistake.

Brodie Cruickshank

I CAME TO CAPE COAST REGULARLY now that the ship was in. George looked over my various reports before I sealed them.

"You realize," he said one day, "that the present government cares nothing for what goes on out here. Now that the slave trade is officially over, I think they would like to shut us down. Anything, anything at all, that you can do while you're on leave would be very helpful. Call on the Colonial office, tell Forster to keep up all his connections. Somehow we have to get it across to them that England will be very sorry if she removes her flags and her officers from this coast. We *must* remain here and we need more money. When I was in London one of those armchair travellers at the Colonial office asked why on earth I needed money for entertaining these 'nigger chiefs'? Why should I give them presents? Surely a show of power would be far more effective than a waistcoat or an iron skillet. It was all I could do to keep from hitting him, hitting all of them, lounging around in their leather armchairs, sniffing brandy, talking about 'the good old days.' Of course I'm a Scot — and you are as well. We don't have the right accents. We came up the hard way. Do what you can. I've tried to explain our position, yet again, but I'm sure a 'man on the spot' would help to emphasize our cause. It's our *duty* to stay, but they can't see it."

Brodie: I stole one of Letitia's handkerchiefs; it smelled of her eau de cologne.

Letty (to Brodie): "I drink such quantities of tea, I'm sure I slosh when I walk. Fifteen cups yesterday and the Dry Season not really begun. I take it in the Russian manner now, clear, with a slice of lemon. So refreshing. I do rather limit the biscuits, however; I have a horror of getting fat. Mrs. Bailey has no such qualms, but then, she was fat to begin with. Have you met her consort? He is a very small man, small and wiry. When they walk together on Sunday, he looks like some kind of child beside her, a child with bowed legs and an ancient, suntanned face. Or maybe she's a small ship with the figurehead walking along beside, instead of up front where it belongs. I expect you'll see quite a lot of them on the voyage home."

One day I heard a lot of screaming down on the beach, just below the battlements where I was standing. A girl was being dragged into the water by a group of girls and women. Other girls ran along beside, pelting her with red mud. They tumbled her over in the waves.

I rushed to find Isaac.

"They are going to drown her!"

Isaac laughed.

"No, Madame. Dis ting is good ting."

"Not good for the girl, surely. Can't we do something?"

"Look, Madame, she be laugh."

And it was true. They were dragging her out of the water now and she was laughing.

"Well," said Brodie, when I told him, "she must be pregnant."

"Pregnant? That little girl?"

"They weren't hurting her, Letty. They are making sure the pregnancy will go well. They do this to keep the bad luck away. Later, a fetish woman will tie all sorts of charms and amulets on her and mutter some spells."

"And all that will keep her safe."

"Perhaps. It won't hurt, at any rate. We all have our customs and superstitions. In Scotland, a groom is sometimes tarred and feathered and paraded though the village streets on the night before his wedding. And many a farmer's field, to this day, has a wee triangular bit left unplowed — 'the devil's share.'"

Letty

I DID NOT TELL ANYONE about the other dolls I had received; George only knew about the first one. He assumed the matter had been taken care of. Three were locked up in my secret drawer, along with other things. I did not tell anyone about the person who came at night and stood outside my door, anyone except Mrs. Bailey, who, being such a practical person, just thought I was having some kind of hysterical fit and she was not to tell.

I wasn't so much afraid anymore as anxious to see what would happen next. Perhaps I had written so much about frightening things in my novels that I had made myself immune to horror. I said to myself, *Someone is doing this in jest, to see how the "'Bronie lady" will react.* I did quiz Isaac, but he insisted no one gets by him in the night. On the other hand, I have heard the merchants talk of how their watchmen do more snoring than watching.

Where could someone hide during the day and not be seen?

There were always vultures wheeling up above the town.

George

SUCH A CARRY-ON WHEN I THREATENED to throw her drops overboard. "I'll die, George. I'll fall dead at your feet."

It's not that I knew what was in the bottle; I just didn't like the idea of dependency.

Brodie: She mentioned her drops one day; she said they were for "an old complaint."

Mr. Freeman

THEY SAID YOU COULD SMELL THE SLAVE SHIPS when they were a mile out. My poor father! Sold to the highest bidder, a strong young boy. And sold again in the West Indies. His teeth examined, his spine, between his legs. He spoke no English, but soon learned all he needed to know: "Sah." "Yes, Sah." "Mastah." And then, one day, when he accompanies his master to England, when he steps on English soil, he is free. Or so the story goes. Free to go where? Free to do what? What saved him was the fact that his master was an amateur botanist, and kind, as masters go. He became an undergardener and then moved up. What saved him was the love of a good woman, a widow with three sons.

He was always cold — wore a muffler at home. "I'm only warm when I'm working," he said. He had a soft voice, different from the voices out here. It had a lilt to it, which made him sound happy even when he was not.

Soon the Harmattan would begin in a fog of red dust. Hmm. An idea for a sermon, perhaps? The soul's Dry Season, thirsting for refreshment. Yes. I must write it down before I forget it. God's lessons are everywhere — if only one pauses to pay attention. "Blessed are they who do hunger and thirst after Righteousness."

I thought I might just stop at Mr. Swanzy's along the way home; his cook was chopping the heads off chickens as I came by earlier. Strange how they rush about with their heads cut off. Another idea for a sermon? Why, ideas are falling on me as thick as rain. Thomas, you are inspired this afternoon, truly inspired.

Letty

AT THE LAST CHAPEL SERVICE I ATTENDED, Mr. Freeman gave a sermon about dust. It had to do with the coming Harmattan. He spoke in ringing tones for a few minutes, then the interpreter stood up and he sat down. Then Mr. Freeman up again, then down, and the interpreter up. Up. Down. Up. Down. I'm sorry to say it reminded me of a Punch and Judy show. All we needed was the hitting and the little dog. The choir looked splendid in their blue sashes.

George: Excellent sermon Mr. Freeman. I am always pleased to see you using topics from the world as we know it out here.

Mr. Freeman: Thank you, Mr. Maclean. Next week my topic is chickens.

I didn't mean to laugh.

Mr. Freeman

ONE DAY, MRS. MACLEAN MENTIONED she had taught their gardener to read when she was young.

"Was he black?"

"No, but it saddened me that there was someone I knew who was unable to enjoy the world of books."

"And yet you are not saddened by the children here, who cannot read or write."

"Don't pester me, Mr. Freeman. I've told you once, I've told you twice, I made certain commitments before I left England and I must fulfill them before I can think of anything else."

(Another weeping woman, another Byronic hero, another broken heart, another tomb. What rubbish! She sent me a basket of fruit when I was indisposed — but to give of herself?)

Letty

THAT EVENING I ASKED GEORGE what he really thought of the missionaries, not just Mr. Freeman, but missionaries in general.

"I think they do fine work with little reward."

"Well, wouldn't they say their reward is in Heaven? Do you want to know what I think? I think sometimes these worthies resemble the serpent in the Garden of Eden."

"Letty!"

"Aren't they offering Christianity the way the serpent offered the apple? And then when they take it and eat of it thereof, or whatever the Bible says, they discover Sin. They discover Shame."

"They offer redemption; we are all tainted with Original Sin."

"All right. He makes them ashamed and then he tells them to cover up, to abandon their gods and fetishes and Jesus-God will forgive them everything, Jesus-God being sort of like a Heavenly George Maclean, only without the uniform and without the fear of fines. He *introduces* the concept of sin so that they can be saved from sin. Doesn't sound strange to you?"

"You are a casuist."

"No. But since coming here I've been thinking a lot, more than I've ever thought before, about missionaries. Why do we want these people to be Christian?

"Because of the civilizing influence of Christianity and Christian precepts."

"And then what? Once they cover up, get rid of excess wives, ban the old gods, declare themselves for Christ, will they be better off?"

"Of course. They live in spiritual squalor and it keeps them from progressing."

"George, for two centuries the people here witnessed the slave trade. Weren't those mostly Christians who carried it out? Do you think they can easily make the distinction between one kind of

Christian and another?"

"Many of the Africans helped in the slave trade as well."

"Of course they did; they learned from the Europeans."

"There was slavery here long before we came."

"You're impossible!"

"I'm tired. Let's continue this another time."

"Of course."

Letty

THE BACKING ON THE MIRROR IN MY BEDROOM had tarnished in places; it gave back a spotted reflection. Even without constant rain — it was very sporadic now — the humidity tarnished everything. Twice a week the prisoners polished all the cutlery and plate and I saw to the backs of my brushes, a present from the Misses Lance. Brodie told me the story of a silver statue of St. James that the Portuguese had sent to Elmina when they controlled the Castle. It turned black almost as soon as it was unpacked and frightened the natives to death. They thought it was a devil.

Mr. Freeman

HOLINESS IS HAPPINESS. There is joy in salvation. I must get that across to them. The joy!

Letty

I ASKED BRODIE IF HE WOULD UNDERTAKE a commission for me; a few books to use as prizes for the children as they advanced in their studies. Nothing offensive, just books with lots of pictures and a few words. Bible stories would be best, but, barring that, stories of animals. I was going to suggest to Mr. Freeman that we inaugurate a Prize Day in the coming year, making it an annual event. I would present the prizes: *G* for GRACIOUS. I also gave Brodie a letter to a physician in London, *not* Dr. Thomson, who was to entertain a special request, "as previously agreed to."

"Do you mind doing these errands?"

"I would do anything for you."

George

FATHER ASKED ME A QUESTION on my last night at Urquhart.

"George, are you happy out there?"

"Content might be a better way to put it. Content to do my duty to my country."

"Your health is suffering for it."

"Not so badly as some."

"Your uncle might be able to find you something else — in a more salubrious climate."

"It's all right, Father, really."

But it wasn't. Did I think Letty would make it better? I had asked her to marry me on an impulse, but what was that impulse? Love — or desperation? There was no instrument up in my cockloft to measure boredom. I think, secretly, I longed for a war, even a minor war, to stir things up. "Tomorrow and tomorrow and tomorrow ..."

Letty wasn't the only one who could quote Shakespeare. Be careful what you wish for.

Isaac

GUBB'NOR COME QUICK! GUBB'NOR COME QUICK!

Letty

(To Brodie): Mrs. Bailey was telling me about the ju-ju stall in the market. She says it is full of disgusting objects. Love potions/hate potions, roots and powders, "things to stick up yer," as she puts it.

Brodie: Sometimes it is the fear that works the magic, not the thing itself.

Letty: And other times?

Brodie: Well, of course there are a multitude of poisonous things, as you know. And things that cure as well. The garden boys, if they slice a leg with their machete, slap on a leaf and the wound stops bleeding in seconds. But when you ask, "Which leaf? Which leaf?" they won't tell you. We need a botanist to make a tour of this coast and write it all down. I expect Thomas Freeman is already doing some research. Superstition, yes, lots of superstition and fetish nonsense, but a lot of practical knowledge too.

Think of all the folk remedies back home amongst the country women. "Simples," they call them, but it's the same idea. And think of Culpepper, how successful he's been.

Letty: We can't just go out and buy poison.

Brodie: Some poisons we can. To kill rats, for instance.

I thought of my drops; how the doctor at St. George's warned me to always dilute the stuff in distilled water. "There is a country saying about this: three to kill a rabbit, five to kill a man. You must be very careful."

George wanted to throw them overboard, yet at the inquest he said he did not know what hydrocyanic acid meant. If he did not know what it meant, why did he tell me it was "too dangerous"?

And who was he to talk? Were those not opium pills he was taking when he was so ill? It was the opium that caused his delirium, his costiveness.

"Ekosua! Ekosua!" he had cried out again and again.

For four nights I lay on a pallet by the bed, afraid to leave him alone, bathing his forehead as he tossed and turned.

Once, he opened his eyes and recognized me.

"Oh, Letty," he said, "what will you do if I should die?"

"My dear," I replied, "if you were to die, it would not be long before I followed you."

That's what I said to him, but I was frightened; what *would* I do? Go back to England on the October boat? The widow Maclean. At least I would have some status, possibly some money. I know that when we married George changed his will to include me, but there was his family as well; bequests to them I'm sure. Perhaps the widow Maclean wouldn't be much better off than L.E.L.

I had not made a will, although Whittington urged me to it. George had already agreed that my money was my own.

After my death he kept up the payments to my mother; it seemed only right. At his death, of course, they ceased. I assume my brother took over.

"Whittington!"

"Family name," I said.

"Are you related to Dick Whittington and his cat?"

I was always surprised when George attempted humour.

Mrs. Bailey

THERE HAD BEEN A BABY GOAT TETHERED somewhat apart from its mother (I reckon it was to be slaughtered in the morning) and its cries had kept me awake. *Maaa* ... And then response: *Maaa* ... Over and over. The baby would call and the mother would respond. "I'm here, I'm here." So I wasn't in a deep sleep when I heard the screams.

I went down to her right away. She was sitting up in bed, eyes wide with terror, nightdress soaked, the sheets as well.

"Letitia. Mrs. Maclean. Whatever is the matter?"

At that she broke into wild sobbing, so I just held her and said, *Shh, Shh,* until she calmed down. Then I changed the sheets while she put on a fresh gown.

"Don't leave me!" she said, clutching my hand.

"I won't leave you; I'll sit on the chair, here, and stay 'til morning. But what was it that frightened you so?"

"For weeks there's been someone outside my door. When I call out, they don't answer. Tonight I decided to open the door, to see who was playing this joke."

"And?"

"And, when I flung open the door, there was no one. No one I could see. And yet someone was there, I could feel it. A presence. Someone was there, I swear it. I ran back into the room and slammed the door. But whatever it was just stood out there. And then it began to laugh."

Although I don't believe in "presences" and all that nonsense, I could see that she was genuinely frightened. And the way she spoke — of the sense of someone invisible standing outside and laughing, made the hairs stand up on the back of me neck.

"Someone wants to harm me."

"I think these are probably just fancies; you are overtired, what with all that nursing of Mr. Maclean and then trying to finish your essays, like. I think that's all it amounts to. And maybe you could hear the baby goat crying down below."

"I heard no baby goat. I heard laughter, from outside my door. *Something* was really out there. Something wishes me ill."

The next night I offered to stay with her again, but she said she was fine now and to say nothing to Mr. Maclean. I had a little chat with Isaac, who had moved his sleeping-mat away from outside Letitia's door. I told him to get back up there and do as he had been told.

Letty

THEY MUST HAVE "MEDICINE" that makes them invisible. But why stand outside my door? Could they not open the locks and simply walk right in? Strangle me or poison me or do whatever it was they intended to do? My eldest niece had given me a small St. Christopher medal on a golden chain. I had never worn it because it seemed silly to do so. But now I took it out of my jewel case and clasped it around my neck. I doubted it would do any good, but it was worth a try. I told myself all this was a trick and I really should consult George — he'd soon find the culprit.

I stayed longer and longer in our shared bedroom, but as soon as I made my way to my own quarters, the presence followed me. Why didn't it attack me there? Why didn't it force its way in? It played with me, like a cat with a mouse. When I looked in the mirror I could see the huge circles under my eyes and yet George saw me as fine.

"Letty, you continue to amaze me. What is your secret? No fever, nothing. And you have even gained a little weight; it suits you. I wish I had a magic carpet so that I could whisk you over to London for one night (and one night only) to show all the doubters how well you are."

"But you were the major doubter, George, were you not?"

"I was."

A drachma is 60 grains or 1/6 of an ounce; a minim, the smallest fluid measure, is 1/60 of a drachma. I measured out my medicine in minims. *Drip. Drip. Drip.*

If I had died in England, what sort of funeral would there have been? Horses with black plumes, women in black bombazine, men with black armbands? Would there be many coaches? L.E.L. is dead! Or would Whittington simply bury me next to Father, say a few chosen words, and be done with it? Who would attend the funeral? Who would provide the funeral spread? My uncle Landon told me that in Yorkshire there has to be a ham or the funeral is incomplete; what would be the culinary equivalent in London? I realized I had only been to one funeral — my father's — which I had to arrange, Mother being prostrate with grief and Whittington still a student. I can't remember what we served. I was holding back my own terrible grief in order to be the dutiful, efficient daughter. I remember little of that. William Jerdan would be there, of course, Bulwer, ditto, the Misses Lance, perhaps even my mother. How strange to think I have not outlived my mother!

Of course George would not be there, for if I had died in England, in the year of our Lord 1838, I would not have been married to George. And, if I had not been married to George, I would not have died so young.

Would my mother become maudlin, tell everyone how she had come to her marriage with £14,000, a saddle horse, and a groom, but her husband had lost everything and she was reduced to taking money from her daughter?

Did my mother weep for me when she learned of my death out here, or did she think only of herself? When I was a small child I had Whittington to play with, but after he went off to school I was left to my own devices. All Mother's affection went to Lizzie, who was born sickly and continued that way until she died. There was no affection left for me.

But my father loved me. As I have said, I used to swing on the gate at Trevor Park and wait for him each evening. He rode his horse (or perhaps it was Mother's horse?) to town and back and I could hear him coming long before I saw him. He'd been to sea as a midshipman. I loved his stories about that time. I loved the books he bought me: *Robinson Crusoe, Sylvester Tramper, The Arabian Nights.*

Then we came down in the world. My mother never forgave him. And it's true that once you have been used to certain things and then have to do without them, it can make you bitter. Far better to rise than to fall.

I was hoping we'd be able to ride on the Coast.

"George, why are there no horses here?"

"They can't survive."

"Why not? Is it the heat?"

"We don't think so, but we don't really know. In other parts of Africa there are horses. Up in the north, where Ibrahim comes from, they are famous for their horses. There is something here that kills them."

"It's unfortunate. How I should love a gallop across the sands. And an officer on a horse looks so ... important, don't you think? One has to literally look up to him. That would be useful when dealing with the natives."

"They would be useful for lots of reasons; but until someone figures out what sickens them, it is useless to bring them here."

I started publishing just two years before my father died, after we moved back to London. William Jerdan lived next door and my cousin showed him some of my verses. He said I had talent; he said he would gladly become my editor and publisher. It was he who came up with the L.E.L. idea. It added mystery, he said. I found out later that a lot of the boys at Oxford and Cambridge fell in love with me because they thought I was a boy!

William Jerdan was married, but unhappy. Whittington needed to go up to Oxford; Lizzie needed medicine; my mother, well, she needed to keep a respectable household. Even so, nearly every evening I had to listen as she told over her beads of complaint. I had to help; I didn't hesitate to help. But it is not a good thing to always have money as the carrot in front of you to keep you writing furiously. It saps you. Not one of my friends knew how little money I kept for myself. If my grandmother Bishop hadn't left me £400, I could not have lived at 22 Hans Place. I don't think Mother or Whittington ever thanked me properly.

Well, Mother would get all the money from the Scott essays. What with that, and George's contribution, she would be quite comfortable.

So — no horses at all to carry me to the graveyard, no graveyard in fact, for I was buried within the Castle walls. *Tramp tramp tramp* went the soldiers when they did their morning parade. Did they ever think of me? *Hic jacet.* George's memorial was quite lovely. I tended to forget that he had an excellent education. Buried in haste. No real funeral at all, a few words from Mr. Topp, a hymn. Brodie organized the interment; George sat in his room, reading the Bible. Two days later he left for a visit to Accra. The *Governor Maclean* sailed for England, carrying my "worldly goods," my Scott essays, my packet of cheerful letters, and the news of my untimely death.

Mr. Freeman's famous letter was also on the ship. Once it was published in *The Watchman* out flew "Rumour with her painted tongues."

I was eating very little. Fruit compote seemed to be the only thing which really appealed to me anymore. I couldn't stand anything fried in palm oil. I was eating very little and yet I felt bloated a great deal of the time. Perhaps it was my turn for the seasoning fever. I also suffered from a series of boils in my left ear, which Mr. Cobbold had to lance. I was horrified to discover there were maggots inside. The doctor said the washboy must have been laying the bed linen over bushes to dry. Flies then laid their eggs there.

"He knows better than to do that; I must have a word with him."

George did not get the boils, but he was very concerned about me. The lancing was painful, but bearable, but the thought of what was in the boils made me quite ill. There were two days when I simply didn't get up at all. Brodie came to inquire, but I sent him away. I looked ridiculous with a big bandage on the side of my head.

Mrs. Bailey came in to keep me company. She said the washboy had been sent away and wasn't it lucky *she* did our petticoats, bodices, and stays or they might have been full of eggs. I suggested she talk about something else.

About every half-hour she felt my head for fever until I finally told her to stop.

"I do *not* have fever, Mrs. Bailey. I'm just a bit upset."

"Do you wish you were goin' home, Mrs. Maclean?"

"My home is here."

"Of course. But you might be feeling a bit homesick, with the ship in and all. I know I'm very anxious to get back to the family. Not looking forward to the voyage, though. Mrs. Topp has given me some remedy for nausea, but I don't know if I dare take it; it's a most peculiar colour."

"I'd take it if I were you. Anything to avoid that awful seasickness."

"Well, I'll give it a try. If it don't kill me, mebbe it will cure me."

Mr. Freeman came to inquire; it was easy to send him away.

Mr. Freeman

I WAS SORRY TO HEAR THAT MRS. MACLEAN was indisposed. I had thought she looked unwell the previous Sunday. I prayed for her, for both her body and her soul. Now that the Dry Season was almost upon us, how ironic it would be if she succumbed to fever.

George

IT WAS STRANGE TO BE EATING DINNER ALONE. I missed her. She had planned a dinner party for the evening before the ship sailed. She loved dinner parties and would be so disappointed if she were ill.

After my own dinner, I had Isaac take a tray in to her and I sat by her and tried to persuade her to eat. She sat in bed, propped up by pillows, and tried to reassure me.

"I will be fine, George. I think it was just the shock, you know, the horror of it. And the heat. It does seem to be getting hotter by the minute."

"Would you care for some ginger beer?"

"Now that sounds like a splendid idea." But when I left, she still had not touched it.

Letty: He gave my cheek a little pat.

"Sleep well."

Letty: There was no one outside the door those nights. That frightened me even more. Did it mean the "presence" had given up, or that some new devilry was planned? No more breathing; no more dolls.

Letty

ON THE THIRD DAY I FELT SO MUCH BETTER that I decided to get up and walk outside along the battlements. When the sea fog lifted I could see the ship, way out, and canoes going back and forth from shore to ship to shore. A great many goods had to be unloaded and some, like the crates of spirits, needed to be guarded until they could be carried to the storerooms. All was bustle in and around the Castle. The merchants each collected the crates that were marked for them and porters carried away the goods on the tops of their heads. I was always amazed at the loads these people could carry. I once saw a boy with three wooden chairs balanced neatly on his head.

Canoes full of coconuts went out to the ship, great hands of bananas and plantain. Crocks of palm oil. Net bags of oranges, lemons, pineapples.

George and Mr. Topp gave orders and consulted lists. The canoe-men shouted to one another, ran at the canoes, gave them a mighty shove, and then, laughing, jumped in.

The sun on the sea made everything glitter and twinkle. It was such a jolly scene, but I could not help but wonder what this had looked like when the cargo was men, women, and children. One by one, in a long line, led out through "The Door of No Return" and packed into the canoes. Mr. Freeman said most had never even seen the sea before.

"This place," said Mr. Freeman, making a sweeping gesture that included the Castle and the sea, "this place is redolent with misery."

I will frankly admit that I had not thought much about the slavery question when I was growing up. Slavery in England had been abolished when I was only five and although I saw black servants in some of the fine homes I visited later, some of the boys and young men dressed beautifully in livery, I just accepted that they were there. Where they came from never entered my mind. I supposed that is one of the reasons I found Mr. Freeman so irritating; he was bound and determined I should feel guilty for such ignorance.

"All dwellings have voices, Mrs. Maclean; this castle is one long cry of agony. Doesn't it affect you, how you live now and how those others lived down below? Imagine terrified creatures crammed so tightly into cells that they could only squat to sleep. I wonder how many would fit into this spacious room, ten times the size of one of those cells. Five hundred?"

I tried not to think about it, or the fact that in a few more days Brodie would leave. No doubt I would even miss Emily Bailey and her knitting needles.

George turned and glanced up; I waved at him and was rewarded with a big smile. I think I could have grown to love that man.

But wasn't it better this way? If this were a novel, I certainly couldn't have written a more dramatic ending. I do feel badly that George came under suspicion. All the fault of Mr. Freeman and apologies were made and somewhat reluctantly accepted. The earlier rumours didn't help and no doubt Mrs. Bailey fanned the fire when she finally got home. I know she suspected me and toward the end gave me many a knowing look as though to say, "You can't fool me, my girl; why not come out with it?" Vomiting, fainting spells, lack of appetite. I suppose, with our Elsie, so fecund, on her mind, she couldn't help but wonder. I thought of that python making its lazy undulating way down the washing pole. How she had screamed. But supposing she hadn't seen the snake, only felt its presence, or heard a faint slithering, what then? Mrs. Bailey had "ocular proof" that her distress was legitimate.

I had the dolls, of course, and a dead bat, but if I told George? I was afraid he would laugh at me, would remember the hysterical letters I sent to Scotland, shake his head, confer with Mr. Cobbold. And so I kept quiet. *If I could only put a face to it*, I thought. *If I could only see what it looked like, however horrible that might be.*

Mr. Freeman

I MEANT NO HARM. I was just trying to reassure any potential female missionaries that Mrs. Maclean did not die of fever or dysentery. I wrote that she was in perfect health the night before and that was true. At dinner she was laughing, quite in fine form, but then she always blossomed when Brodie Cruckshank was around (which was often). She did excuse herself early, but that was not uncommon: "I'll leave you gentlemen now." All rose. Mr. Cruickshank offered to accompany her to her apartments and she accepted; he took up a lamp and they left. Captain Maclean smiled at her most tenderly and said, "I shall be along presently," but Letitia replied, "No, George, you have been working very hard; stay and enjoy yourself. You will be very busy again tomorrow."

And that was the last I saw of her, as, with Brodie carrying the lamp and lighting her way, she disappeared.

George

SHE WAS WEARING SOMETHING WHITE. I have no talent for describing women's dress, but it was something white, and gauzy. I thought for an instant of the huge white moths that beat their wings against the lamps at night. I watched her until they turned a corner.

I did not see her again that evening. Whenever I stayed late at the Mess and indulged a bit in drink, we slept apart.

We did not share morning tea and biscuits when we spent the night in separate apartments, so when I awoke with an aching head and Isaac appeared with only one cup on the tray, of course I gave no thought to Letitia. The *Maclean* was to sail at 11:00 a.m. and there were still last-minute things to be seen to. I was thinking how glad I would be when it was off and things could get back to normal, when I heard screams from above and running feet.

Mrs. Bailey

I WAS UP EARLY (how could I sleep when I was going HOME?) and dressed myself in my travelling costume. My trunks had been taken on board the day before, so there was only my one case and a few odds and ends left out. I decided I would go down to see how Mrs. Maclean was faring after her collapse and met Isaac just as he was coming up the stairs with her tea tray. I was pleased to see how far he had advanced in just eight weeks, remembering the tray cloth and the slices of lemon, now Letitia took her tea in what she called "the Russian fashion."

I liked the good old "English way" myself, strong tea, milk in a milk jug, plenty of sugar. I remembered all them high-born abolitionist ladies refusing to take sugar in their tea because of slavery on the plantations. I suppose they were right to do so, but my mum said she was glad she was just common stuff as she couldn't abide tea without sugar. And how would you keep the babies quiet without them sugar-tits?

Anyway, I took the tray from Isaac and said I would give it to Mrs. Maclean myself, but when I knocked there was no answer. *Perhaps she has taken a sleeping draught,* I thought, *as she was so upset.*

I set the tray down and knocked harder, but there was still no reply, so I pushed at the door, but it would only open a few inches. I pushed harder, but something was hindering my entrance. I shoved with all my might; the door opened and there she was.

Letty: D for Dead.

Brodie Cruickshank

IT HAD BEEN ARRANGED THAT THE VESSEL should sail on the forenoon of the sixteenth of October and I agreed to dine and spend the evening of the fifteenth with the governor and his lady. It was, in every respect, a night to be remembered.

The dinner was excellent and Letty was in fine form. She insisted we call forth Ibrahim and Isaac to congratulate them. We raised a toast to them; they bowed and returned with the sweet and dessert. We toasted the Queen. We toasted Letty for recovering from her indisposition. We toasted George. I was toasted and wished *bon voyage*. The linen was perfectly pressed; the silver and the plate gleamed; the crystal sparkled. It was hard to believe that a few hundred yards away, in the town, people squatted over braziers, making ground-nut stew and eating with their fingers. "Here" was a little bit of England; "there" was Africa. Which was the reality?

I was so pleased when Letty asked if I would light her way to her apartments. She said she had a few more letters she hoped I would undertake to deliver. I had wished for a word or two alone with her, but knew it would be improper for me to suggest it.

"Let us walk along the battlements for a moment," she said. "I do believe it is cooler out here than in my rooms." A cloud passed over the moon.

"I can't avoid envying you a little, the happiness of seeing the dear old country again. You must not forget to call on some of my more particular friends, and assure them that I am happy and in good health."

"Write to me. And you must catch and bottle up the very essence of that great city. Send it to me by the next ship and I shall add it to my medicine chest, indulge in a whiff or two whenever I am lonely."

"I will do that with pleasure."

Letty: I gave a little laugh, which somehow turned into a sob and there I was, collapsed in a puddle of tears and muslin, clinging to his legs like some beggar-woman calling, "Take me with you! Please!"

Brodie: I was astonished and then horrified, and so I did an unforgivable thing: I pried her fingers loose and fled.

Mrs. Bailey: I was just coming from turning down her bed and making sure she had everything she needed for the night. There was Mr. Cruickshank, or Mr. Cruickshank's back, disappearing at a fast clip, and there was Letitia, sunk to the floor and weeping hysterically. I rushed to her at once and asked what on earth had happened. She made little sense, something about a face — I think she said "a face," mebbe it was "a place" or "no place"? but I'm not sure and something about "poor Brodie" and then laughing hysterically — she looked proper wild, she did.

"Did Mr. Cruickshank say something to upset you? Is that it?"

Laughed again — "No, no, it is I who upset him, I who have upset him. Oh, Bailey, lend me your arm, help me to my room. George mustn't see me like this. Hurry. We must hurry."

I half-carried her up to her room and helped her to undress. I even offered to stay with her, although I was not quite finished with my own packing. She had calmed down somewhat, but still gasped as though she couldn't get enough air.

She asked me to leave a candle burning as she knew she wouldn't sleep for a while. I can still see her, propped up on pillows, terribly pale.

"Should I fetch the doctor?"

"'No doctor; it's not a doctor I need. Just go. And thank you for your help.'"

Then, just as I was opening the door.

"Mrs. Bailey. Do you ever hear cries at night? Not the hyrax, but something else?"

"I don't think so, but I sleep very soundly. Once I'm down, I'm down. Mr. Bailey says only the trumpets at Judgment Day would wake me and maybe not even then. But with all this mumbo-jumbo around, perhaps you hear the wails from one of their outlandish ceremonies. Sound carries. Although, with that infernal surf, I'd be surprised you could hear anything from the town."

"I don't think it's from the town." She shrugged. "Oh well, I suppose it's just my overactive imagination."

"I expect so. Good night, Mrs. Maclean."

And those were the last words I ever said to her, poor thing. I should have stayed and tried to find out what had put her in such a state. Somehow I didn't think Mr. Cruickshank was at the root of it, although his running away aroused my suspicions at first. I could hardly go to the governor with what I'd witnessed; he didn't approve of the amount of time she spent with that man. He'd immediately think the worst. I don't like mysteries, myself, want everything aboveboard.

I should have stayed with her; I'll have that on me conscience for the rest of me days.

Mr. Freeman: I was just checking that the watchman was actually watching our building supplies and not just sound asleep on a pile of boards, when I heard someone running along the main path. They did not seem to be coming towards the church and so I didn't bother to investigate. It was only later, given what happened the next day, that I wondered.

George: I felt such an incredible tenderness toward her that night. The way she had gone all out when planning the dinner party, the way she had coped for the past eight weeks without all the refinements she was used to. After she left, we men stayed on talking for quite a while and when I stood up I realized I was quite drunk. I wanted to go to her, to make love to her, to tell her how proud I was of her; but it was past midnight and I knew she would be fast asleep.

Tomorrow, I thought, *tomorrow, after the* Maclean *sails, I will tell her all this.* And so I staggered to my solitary bed.

Letty

I NEVER USED THE FLANNEL, so highly recommended by that awful woman in Eastbourne, as well as by an acquaintance who had a sister living in India. It remained at the bottom of my trunk. I assume it went back to England with the rest of my clothes. Or was everything sorted out by Mrs. Bailey, this for the missionary society, that for Mrs. Topp, something for herself, perhaps? My pretty dresses, my little shoes, my gloves, my parasol. My stays! They are mad for European dress; would George one day meet a woman coming towards him in my travelling cloak? Another dressed in my corsets? Who got my silver-backed brushes? Perhaps it would all be bundled up and taken to the market (except for what Mrs. Bailey chose to keep). "*Bronie Wawu*": a white man has died. A white woman.

George: I left it to Mrs. Bailey to pack away her things. "Take anything that would be useful to you," I said.

Letty: Men do not know how to deal with such things, a dead wife, a dead wife's clothes. That's what neighbour women are for, and female relations. They perform so many of the necessary tasks, of life, of death. Mrs. Bailey had to do it all.

Had I been in London … well, I wasn't.

I wonder who did the honours for the missionary wives — Mrs. Topp? The missionary husbands?

Mr. Freeman was at that last dinner. Before his place I put a large carafe of water and labelled it "Adam's Ale." A bit mean? He took it in good humour.

"Ah, Mrs. Maclean, you know me well!"

"We shall not sleep, but we shall all be changed, in a moment, in the twinkling of an eye …"

Letty

BRODIE TOLD ME THAT WHEN THE OLD KING died and Victoria was
named successor, the talking drums spread the news from one end of
Africa to another in less than a day. Amazing.

What did the drums say about my passing? The governor's lady/
The governor's lady/The governor's lady/is *dead* — da da/*dead* —
da da/*dead*.

Mrs. Bailey washed me, tidied my hair, put me in my pretty dress.
Then I was wrapped in white linen and placed (not by George) in a
simple wooden coffin made of odum wood. There were always coffins available in one of the warehouses. Then carried (not by George)
to the side of the grave.

I was buried that evening within the precincts of the Castle. Mr.
Topp read the funeral service.

The whole of the residents assisted at the solemn ceremony. Except
George. ·

George

MRS. BAILEY, RED-FACED AND PANTING, in her hideous wrapper of market cloth: "Mr. Maclean! Mr. Maclean!"

"Sir ... she's ... taken some sort of fit. Come quick."

I was feeling the worse for my overindulgence of the night before and resented being burst in upon like this. And I am ashamed to say that I wondered for a minute if this was one of Letty's hysterical episodes. After all, the ship was about to sail and she could not help but think of home; but there was real terror in Mrs. Bailey's face, so I called for Isaac to summon Mr. Cobbold and went immediately to Letty's room.

The louvres were still shut in her bedroom and there was the lingering smell of a candle recently snuffed out. Why was she writing by candlelight? Was this another of her romantic impulses; had she coaxed some wax to drop upon the letters as though she were composing them at midnight and not at breakfast-time?

Mrs. Bailey had left her where she had fallen, although pushed along a bit because of the opening of the door. She was still in her dressing-gown, one hand uncurled where the bottle had been. Mrs. Bailey said she had removed it and placed it on the dressing-table.

Her eyes were wide open, staring, but held so little of life they could have been the eyes of a statue.

I picked her up in my arms and placed her on the bed. Mrs. Bailey opened the louvres and broad bands of morning sunlight lay across her body. Mr. Cobbold came rushing in and attempted a purgative, but it just ran down the sides of her mouth. In another few minutes she was dead. No sigh, just a slight relaxation of her limbs.

Letty: He was calling my name, but it sounded like a voice from the bottom of a well:

Leh-ty Leh-ty

And then nothing.

George: I had seen death before — many times; but this was my wife; this was the woman I had brought out here and promised to protect.

An accidental overdose: that's what the doctor decided at our hasty inquest. I stated that I had not known hydrocyanic acid was prussic acid; how could I have known? I'm not a chemist.

"Where is the beaker of water?" I asked, for Letty was very careful with those drops; I'd seen her counting out loud as she measured them into a beaker of water many times.

Mrs. Bailey did not know. Mr. Cobbold thought he might have used it while attempting to revive her.

"But where is it?"

My companions shifted uncomfortably. Someone put a hand on my arm to steady me ...

Isaac and Ibrahim were peering around the door. I shouted at them: "Get back to work, you lazy niggers!" Was sorry about that later and told them so. But now news of Letty's death would fly around the town in no time. Now the gossip would begin.

The hand on my arm once again. "Come away, George. For a little while at least." I allowed myself to be taken to my rooms and a tumbler of rum was set before me.

It was decided there would be no autopsy. Accidental — or deliberate — it was clear that the drops had killed her. Hadn't Mrs. Bailey sworn that she found the bottle in Letty's hand?

Mrs. Bailey: There *was* a bottle in her hand. Them drops, I think, but I'm not sure.

George: Her eyes were wide open, but when I called her name, she did not respond. Mr. Cobbold, having been told about the bottle, which Mrs. Bailey said she had removed from Letty's hand and placed on the bureau, called for it at once and exclaimed: "Prussic acid! She has taken prussic acid!" And then he turned to me. "Did you know she had this stuff?"

George: "I knew she took drops, but I had no idea this was prussic acid.

Mr. Cobbold: Hydrocyanic acid — same thing. My God!

George: She was still alive, but barely. The doctor tried emetics, tried everything he could think of, but she did not respond. Her weak pulse grew weaker and then she died. There were one or two open letters on her desk, the second one barely begun. "My dear Whittington, if it will not be too dear, could you pl—" She must have been gripped with an intense pain, seized the drops, and, in her distraught state, accidentally taken an overdose. The alternative didn't bear thinking about.

Mrs. Bailey: He sat there, holding her dead hand, murmuring over and over, "Oh, Letty, oh, my poor girl."

Brodie Cruickshank: An inquest was called that afternoon and the verdict was set down, "Accidental overdose of prussic acid." Mr. Cobbold decided against an autopsy and George concurred. In the early days after her death I was inclined to agree with the verdict, but later I began to doubt that this was what really happened. It is a fact that she took drops and no doubt that she suffered from intermittent pain and had done most of her life. But she *always* mixed the drops with water; she said so and George had seen her do it many times. Would she really have been in such distress she'd drink directly from the bottle? And if not, where was the tumbler? She always kept a carafe of distilled water and a tumbler on her dressing table. Were they there? Were they examined? When I quizzed Mrs. Bailey she couldn't remember. When I asked her why she stopped to take the bottle out of Letty's hand when time was of the essence, she didn't know. When I asked if there was the smell of almonds on Letty's breath she couldn't say, she never got that close. Yet she was the one who closed her eyes.

So the verdict of accidental overdose was based solely on the fact that her eyes were dilated. In situations of extreme terror the pupils are also dilated. I think she died of a heart attack; I think something frightened her to death. The night before, when she cried out to me, I should have insisted she tell me what was wrong. It wasn't mere homesickness that troubled her; there was something more.

Mr. Freeman: Of course I wasn't invited to sit in on the inquest, even though I was probably the most knowledgeable about poisons. I would have asked to examine the bottle; I would have wanted to compare it with the other bottles in her medical chest. When I heard later that both her personal physician, Dr. Thompson, and the pharmacist who made up her medicines for Africa (the Queen's pharmacist, no less) insisted they had never prescribed prussic acid, I hoped more questions would be asked. Someone said the label had been altered and "hydrocyanic acid" had been substituted for what it originally said.

Add to that the fact that we only have Mrs. Bailey's word that the bottle was found in Mrs. Maclean's hand and I'm inclined to think she died of something else. Or was killed. It's not impossible, is it? Not by Captain Maclean; he could have smothered her with a pillow any night he chose. Perhaps the country wife: there were rumours she was back in Cape Coast Town.

Or suicide: she deliberately poisoned herself. But that would be a great sin. And why would she do that when she had everything to live for? Even without my unfortunate letter, which never intended any harm, I understood from Mr. Topp, who received a letter from Brodie Cruickshank, that the Literary World of London was up in arms. And unfortunately, because of my letter, really just a monthly report that was published in *The Watchman*, Mr. Maclean was the primary suspect. But there were letters, too, that she had sent to her friends ...

George: Teasing letters. Do you think she would have shown them to me if those remarks were meant in earnest?

Brodie: As regards the cheerful letters, some said they were just a brave attempt to convince her friends — perhaps even to convince herself — that she was all right.

Brodie Cruickshank

I WAS STAYING THE NIGHT AT MR. TOPP'S BUNGALOW and this is where
I went after leaving Letty and the Castle. We were having a hasty breakfast the next morning when a negro servant rushed in. We thought he
said, "Mr. Maclean is dead," which was terrible news, but not altogether
surprising as he hadn't been well since his return. But then the servant,
catching his breath, said, "No be gubbnor, sah, be missus."

I shall never forget the sight of her lying on the bed, hair unbound, in
a lacy dressing gown. Her eyes were wide open and completely blank,
the pupils much dilated. The doctor was shaking his head as we arrived.

George Maclean held himself together until after the inquest, then
he sank into a chair and wept. I asked him if I should arrange the
funeral service and the burial. He nodded and wrung my hand, too
overcome to speak.

The skies opened up just after the service and I stood alone all evening while the soldiers dug her grave. How terrible it was, the flickering torches, the busy workers, the rain coming down. Even with
the sound of the rain, I could hear them screwing down the lid of her
coffin. I felt I must stand there until the work was done; I owed that
to Letitia, who had been so good to me. And I felt guilt, terrible guilt,
that I had left her in such distress, had run away. George stayed in his
room, poor fellow, too distraught to do anything at all.

He left for Accra two days later and did not return for a week. Mr.
and Mrs. Bailey stayed on for several months.

Letty: No great fuss for the gubbnor's lady. No discharge of muskets,
no wailing of women, no shaving of heads. I would have liked some
extravagant ceremony: no fuss for my wedding, no fuss for my "dead-
ing" — I was simply wrapped like a parcel, placed in the coffin, and
lowered into the red earth. More earth was thrown on top and then an
oiled cloth was placed over the grave until a slab could be put there.

Brodie: Just as I was turning away — in spite of my heavy cloak I had been soaked to the skin — Thomas Freeman appeared, Bible in hand. He began to cry out in a loud voice, "The Lord gave and the Lord hath taken away; blessed be the name of the Lord!" Then George, looking like a madman, came rushing down the stairs from his quarters.

"Get rid of him! For God's sake send him away!"

Brodie: I sailed the next day. George shook my hand in a distracted manner, thanked me for all my help. I never heard him mention her name again, except in the letters he sent to defend himself against charges of neglect or even worse. He died of dysentery in 1847. I was one of his executors and he left me fifty pounds.

He wished to be buried next to his wife and this was done, their coffins almost touching. *Hic jacet.*

Letty

LETTY: WHEN THEY FOUND ME I WAS WEARING my prettiest peignoir, pale, peach-coloured silk with ecru lace at neckline and cuffs. I had not yet done up my hair, but all traces of the night's weeping had been sponged away. I did not look ugly or contorted in any way. Except that my eyes were open; I could have been sleeping — had the governor's lady chosen for some bizarre reason to emulate the natives and sleep on the floor?

Mrs. Bailey was wrong; I wasn't pregnant; I was poisoned.

George: There would have been a note, and I swear to you, there was never a harsh word between us. Those letters that her friends dined out on in London, were playfully meant. Otherwise, why would she bring them to me unsealed and laughing, insist that I read them? Her old pain had suddenly returned — that's the whole story. In her distress, she grabbed the bottle and put it to her lips.

I *have* to believe that. I stopped asking myself, "Where was the beaker, where was the carafe of distilled water?"

I am a very ordinary man, but I fell in love with an extraordinary woman. Yes! I loved her. Not like one of her heroes, perhaps, but the love was there. Do you think she knew that? That I loved her?

Letty: Do you think he knew — that I was falling in love with him? A little more time, even a few months, would have been nice. Well, I was saved the ghastly voyage home, wasn't I? And I finished the first of the Scott essays, that's something.

I wonder if my daughter, Laura, ever knew that I was her mother? Would William Jerdan have told the family, whoever they are, wherever they are?

I couldn't have borne the disgrace, the scandal. And I would have made a terrible mother. Out here, a woman is disgraced if she does not produce at least a gaggle of little ones; she can be cast aside if she doesn't.

George had a son — his name is Kwesi; George never knew I knew. Mr. Freeman "accidentally" let it slip. The village is not that far from here, at Agona Junction.

"Accidentally" let it slip, just as I "accidentally" took an overdose of hydrocyanic acid. As if I would! And *if* I did, I would have had the decency to leave a note instead of an unfinished letter to my brother: I owed him that, my St. George, my rescuer.

Mr. Freeman: She was a silly woman. Still, she would be missed.

Brodie: I shouldn't have run away from her that night. At the very least I could have returned to the Mess and asked George to see to her.

Letty: The door opened slowly and a young woman came into my room. She was wearing Adinkra cloth, as though she were in mourning; her head was shaved. I could not really see her face for the lamp was sputtering and about to go out.

"Who are you? Who let you in here? What do you want?"

She said nothing, but walked over to the dressing table, picked up my brushes and combs, examined them, put them down. Picked up my unguents and creams. My drops. Everything examined, with her back to me, everything handled and set down.

"Ekosua?" I whispered. "Are you Ekosua?"

She turned and smiled, but said nothing.

"What do you want with me? Why are you tormenting me?"

She picked up my stays, which were hanging over a screen; she fingered the lace on my peignoir.

"Do you want that? Take it! Take it! Take whatever you want and then leave me alone."

She came to the end of the bed.

"I want *you*."

And then she left.

Although my heart was racing and I could barely stand, I felt I must go to George as quickly as possible. George would tell me the truth about Ekosua and then he would get rid of her.

But the door wouldn't open; something was holding it shut from the other side.

I felt so ill; it was as though I had swallowed a stone. If only I could get to George.

Someone wanted me dead. Or something. Something steadied my hand, something said, "Take this. Now. It will be better this way."

There was some talk of sending me home with the ship, but George said, "No, she is my wife. She will lie here in the Castle and someday I will lie beside her."

He cut off a lock of my hair. It was in the back of his watchcase and was taken out and buried with him. The watch was sent to his younger brother, James.

And still the hyrax screams at night, and still the drummers drum. And still the ghost mothers search for their children calling, "Come. Come. Come. Come. Come." And still the wind in the palm trees rattles the leaves like bones.

Mr. Cobbold: "Incautiously administered by her own hand."

George: I should have thrown that bottle overboard, but when I threatened to do this, she begged me not to: "George, I beg you; I shall die without my drops!"

I didn't know they were prussic acid; how could I know?

Mr. Freeman: Three drops to kill a rabbit; five drops to kill a man.

Brodie: I think I was a little bit in love with her. She said she *felt* more than other people. "It's as though I lack some outer covering that would protect me; this is both my blessing and my curse."

Letty: Did George weep? Did Brodie? Did my little girl, wherever she is, give an involuntary shudder and her mother or governess say, "Someone just walked over your grave."

Mrs. Bailey: I would've liked that bottle, just as a curiosity, you know, but it disappeared.

Isaac: *Onyame N'aa*. God, He never sleep.

Epilogue

LETTY: ONCE UPON A TIME ... or how do the French say it? *Il y a une fois ...*

Once upon a time there was a plain but clever little English girl who rolled her hoop and kept her nose in a book at the same time. Her neighbour was Mr. William Jerdan, editor of the *Literary Review*.

And once upon a time there was a sturdy little Scots boy, a "douce laddie," but rather solitary, but who dreamt of doing some great thing ...

They grew up; they married; they died.

How sobering to be summed up like that in seven words, two commas, and a full stop. But I tell you this, if I could have roused myself from the fog that was so rapidly rising, if I had only had the chance to whisper to George before I died, I would have pressed his hand and whispered simply this:

"No regrets, my dear, no regrets."

Afterword

ONE SATURDAY VANCOUVER MORNING, in 1964, back in the days when mail was still delivered on Saturdays, a blue aerogramme was dropped through the mail slot in our front door. This act changed our lives.

We were all sitting in the kitchen at the back of the house, enjoying our usual lazy Saturday "Full English" breakfast: bacon, fried eggs, tomato, mushrooms, and fried sourdough rye from Ernie's Austrian Bakery, when we heard the mailman's step on the porch.

"I'll get it," my husband said, and headed down the hall.

He didn't return right away and I began to worry that there had been some bad news about his parents (in England) or mine (in the United States). When he did come back, he was holding an open air-letter and he had a funny smile on his face. "How would you like to go to Africa?" he said.

That letter came at just the right moment in our lives. We had immigrated to Canada in 1959 and now owned a large if rather dilapidated house in Kitsilano and were parents of not just the infant daughter we had brought with us, who had just celebrated her fifth birthday, but another little girl, aged two and a half. My husband had a good job teaching art on the east side and I was a full-time mother and part-time graduate student, working slowly toward an advanced degree. Everything was fine, and yet we were feeling restless; too "settled," perhaps, and had even sent inquiries to the Northwest Territories to see if they had any jobs available. An interview had been set up for the end of the month.

The letter was from a former tutor of my husband's back in England. He had been seconded to the Kwame Nkrumah University of Science and Technology outside Kumasi in Ghana and his two years were up; he'd been asked to suggest a replacement. He got our address from an old Christmas card.

We sent a cable saying YES YES YES and asked for more information. We cancelled the interview with the man from Yellowknife, put my Ph.D. on hold and in August we left for two years in Africa. The month before I had discovered I was three months pregnant, but that is another story.

We took a train across Canada, then a short flight to see my mother (my father had been ill for some time and died in June), a train to New York City where we boarded a ship for England to see his parents and then another ship, the MV *Apapa* from Liverpool to Takoradi. The girls loved all the travelling and were exactly the right ages to be excited by all these adventures.

The voyage out took two weeks, calm the whole time, but hot once we were round the Bay of Biscay. We stopped twice, once in the Gambia, where heavily armed soldiers brought bars of gold boullion on board, and once at Freetown, Sierra Leone, to take on a crowd of deck passengers: ten pounds to Lagos! I felt as though we were in some old movie or a Graham Greene novel — all the swirls of colour, the babble of languages, the heat. We finally arrived on our daughter's third birthday, and halfway to Kumasi we stopped at an outdoor café (The Don't Mind Your Wife Chop Bar) for snacks and cool drinks. She remembers the monkeys in the trees.

The Kwame Nkrumah University of Science and Technology, which became just the University of Science and Technology after Nkrumah was overthrown in a virtually bloodless coup, had connections to a small resort at Cape Coast, where one could, for a very small fee, stay on the beach in small chalets the pink colour of coconut ice and just relax. It was during Easter Break in 1965, that we went down. As well as swimming — careful of the undertow — making sandcastles, and enjoying fresh fish, we visited both Cape Coast Castle and Elmina. This was the first time that I saw the graves of George Maclean and Letitia Landon. Our guide, a young policeman, explained that Mrs. Maclean had been a famous English lady who wrote books and a mystery still surrounded her death. I'd never heard of Letitia Landon, but I was a writer and I liked mysteries, so I made a metal note of this. It took me almost forty years to get back to her.

Beginning a research project is exciting, but also dangerous, unless you exercise some self control. It's a bit like sitting next to a big bowl of peanuts; can you limit yourself to one or two? You find out a lot of interesting stuff that may not have anything to do with your book and when you look at your watch half a day has gone by! You learn to rein yourself in, but not too tightly.

All four of the principal characters in *Local Customs* are real people: George Maclean, Letitia Landon, Brodie Cruickshank, and Thomas Birch Freeman. Cape Coast Castle still stands — I have walked in the bedroom where Letty died. Some years ago there was a movement to either tear it down or renovate it and open it as a hotel. Fortunately, neither of these ideas got very far off the ground. It is now a World Heritage Site, as is Elmina. The wind in the palm trees still rattles the leaves like bones.

Acknowledgements

There are many people I ought to thank, but most especially the secretary of the Methodist Church of England, who wrote me a letter that gave me access to a reader's ticket for the archives at the School of Oriental and African Studies, where the papers of Thomas Birch Freeman are kept; the Canada Council, who gave me a grant a long time ago toward the first leg of the journey; the Rare Book Room at The British Library where, on my very last day in Britain, I found a small pamphlet by a doctor in 1830s London who was using hydrocyanic acid to help alleviate the pain of Female Complaints; Wendy Ewart who acted as chaffeuse and old friend on our wonderful trip to the Highlands; Sally Millar Marlow for her trip to St. Mary's, Bryanston Square, and her sketch of the same; Alice Munro and Stephen O'Shea, both of whom encouraged me when no publisher would; as always, my cheerful typist, Carole Robertson; last of all, special thanks to Ian, who got me there in the first place.

More Great Reads from Dundurn

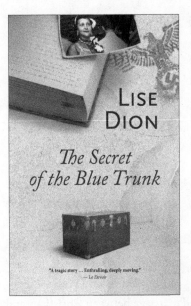

The Secret of the Blue Trunk
Lise Dion;
translated by Liedewy Hawke
978-1459704510
$21.99

In this true story, Armande Martel, a young nun from Quebec, is arrested by the Germans in 1940 during a stay at her religious order's mother house in Brittany. She spends the war years in a German concentration camp. After her return to Canada, she leaves the Church, finds the love of her life in Montreal, and adopts Lise Dion. Growing up, Lise is familiar with only a few facts of her mother's past. It's when she clears her mother's small apartment after her death that Lise Dion discovers the key to the blue trunk, which was always locked. This key unlocks the mystery of Armande's early life, and Lise decides to write *The Secret of the Blue Trunk*.

Outcasts
A Love Story
Susan M. Papp
978-1554884223
$29.99

In this story of love and loss, Tibor Schroeder, a Christian and reservist in the Hungarian forces allied with Nazi Germany, and Hedy Weisz, a young Jewish woman, meet and fall in love during the Second World War — a time when romantic liaisons and marriage between Christians and Jews were not only frowned upon, but against the law. Not knowing of the dangers that await them, Tibor and Hedy pledge their lives to each only to be torn apart when Hedy and her family are herded into one Nagyszollos' ghettoes. Twenty-five years pass before the lovers are finally reunited in Canada. Based on true events, this sprawling love story of hope, courage, and redemption will stay with readers long after finishing the book.

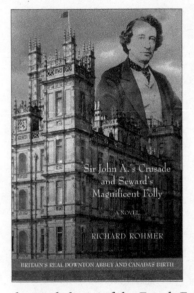

Sir John A.'s Crusade and Seward's Magnificent Folly
Richard Rohmer
978-1459709850
$19.99

In late 1866, John A. Macdonald and other Fathers of Confederation arrived in London to begin discussions with Britain to create Canada. Macdonald and two of his colleagues stayed briefly at Highclere Castle in Hampshire, the stately home of the Fourth Earl of Carnarvon, Britain's colonial secretary. Those are the facts. Today Highclere Castle is widely known as the real-life location for the popular television series *Downton Abbey*. In Richard Rohmer's novel, Macdonald talks with Carnarvon at Highclere about legislation to give Canada autonomy, the danger of Irish Fenian assassination plots, and the proposed American purchase of Alaska from Russia. Later, back in London, a fire partially destroys Macdonald's hotel room, and the future prime minister, trying to curb his fondness for alcohol, woos and marries his second wife, Agnes. In the end, Macdonald wins the passage of the British North America Act but fails in his bid for Alaska when U.S. Secretary of State William Seward buys that strategic territory. Secret deals, romance, and international intrigue all figure in this rousing tale of historical speculation set on the eve of the birth of a nation.

Mary Janeway
The Legacy of a Home Child
Mary Pettit
978-1554884131
$22.99

Mary Janeway is the story of a little girl's childhood while living on a farm as a domestic servant in the late 1800s. Based on extensive historical research, Mary's story begins in Scotland where family circumstances lead to her being sent to Canada as a home child. Separated from her siblings Mary, at age eight, is sent to a farm near Inner Jacques family "needed a girl." Her story bring details of hardship and deprivation experien thousands of young people sent to Canada be